About the author

Sharon Booth writes co... paranormal romantic comedies. Happy endings guaranteed for her main characters, though she likes to make them work for it.

Sharon is a member of the Society of Authors and the Romantic Novelists' Association, and an Authorpreneur member of the Alliance of Independent Authors. She has been a KDP All-Star Author on several occasions.

She loves watching Doctor Who and Cary Grant movies, adores horses and hares, and enjoys strolling around harbours and old buildings. Take her to a castle, an abbey, or a stately home and she'll be happy for hours. She admits to being shamefully prone to crushes on fictional heroes.

Her stories of romance, community, family and friendship are set in pretty villages and quirky market towns, by the sea or in the countryside. Sometimes they feature ordinary men and women, sometimes they feature witches or other magical beings.

If you love heroes and heroines who are flawed but kind, who do the best they can no matter what sort of challenges they face, you'll love Sharon's books.

Books by Sharon Booth

There Must Be an Angel
A Kiss from a Rose
Once Upon a Long Ago
The Whole of the Moon

Summer Secrets at Wildflower Farm
Summer Wedding at Wildflower Farm

Resisting Mr Rochester
Saving Mr Scrooge

Baxter's Christmas Wish
The Other Side of Christmas
Christmas with Cary

New Doctor at Chestnut House
Christmas at the Country Practice
Fresh Starts at Folly Farm
A Merry Bramblewick Christmas
Summer at the Country Practice
Christmas at Cuckoo Nest Cottage

Belle, Book and Candle
My Favourite Witch
To Catch a Witch
Will of the Witch

How the Other Half Lives: Part One: At Home
How the Other Half Lives: Part Two: On Holiday
How the Other Half Lives: Part Three: At Christmas

Winter Wishes at The White Hart Inn

New Doctor at Chestnut House

Bramblewick 1

SHARON BOOTH

Copyright © 2017 Sharon Booth.

Paperback published 2022
Cover design by Green Ginger Publishing

The moral rights of the author have been asserted.
All rights reserved. No part of this publication may be reproduced, stored in any retrieval system, or transmitted in any form, or by any means electronic, mechanical, photocopying, recording or otherwise, without the prior written permission of the publishers.

This book is a work of fiction. Names, characters, businesses, organisations, places and events other than those clearly in the public domain, are either the product of the author's imagination or are used fictitiously. Any resemblances to actual persons, living or dead, is entirely coincidental.

ISBN: 9798364112392

For the hardworking staff of the NHS, with thanks

Chapter 1

Anna Gray glanced around the kitchen and gave a satisfied smile. No one could complain that it wasn't sparkling clean, and she knew the same applied to every room in the house. At least when the new tenant arrived he wouldn't be able to moan about the state of the place.

She glanced at the clock on the wall, feeling a familiar pang as she did so. It was a novelty clock in the shape of a chicken. She'd bought it for her dad, who'd kept hens in a run at the back of the garden.

'Nothing like a freshly-laid egg,' he'd say every morning, as he returned from his daily visit to the hen house, basket over his arm.

He'd eaten a boiled egg every morning for breakfast, complete with bread and butter cut into 'soldiers', just as she'd had when she was a child. He hadn't thought much to her later preference for a bowl of cereal. He took it as a personal insult to his beloved hens, however much she assured him she was just as fond of 'the girls' as he was.

Sadly she wondered what he'd think to the fact that she'd sold them all to a neighbour. She'd had no choice really. Her father was gone, she was moving out, and the house was to be let to the new doctor in the village, on the understanding that if he decided to stay he would buy it.

Anna had no doubt that he would indeed decide to stay. Why would anyone want to leave Bramblewick? It was a picturesque village, nestling in a valley, deep in the wild and beautiful North Yorkshire Moors, and although it didn't have much in the way of facilities it was so picture postcard perfect that she couldn't imagine wanting to live anywhere else. Except... Except that's exactly what she would be doing in a few weeks.

After giving the kitchen one last check, she moved into the hallway and reached for her jacket and boots, having decided to go to the shop to get some basic provisions to welcome the new doctor. Maybe she'd even get a bunch of flowers to brighten the place up if Maudie had any left on sale. She felt restless and needed to get out of the house.

'Morning, Anna. All set for your new visitor?'

She lost count of how many people asked her that as she walked to Maudie's shop. Her friends and neighbours were full of sympathetic smiles and poorly disguised curiosity. It was understandable. Her father had been the village doctor for over thirty years, and they'd all known and loved him. When he'd died, it had been a massive shock to them all—not least Anna herself, who'd been trying to persuade him to retire and take things easy for a long time.

'Plenty of time to relax when I'm dead,' he'd tell her, smiling and tapping the side of his nose.

Well, death had come upon him suddenly and without warning. She sometimes wondered if that was the kindest thing. At least he hadn't suffered any pain or had to live with the knowledge that time was slipping away from him. On the other hand, he'd had no time to say goodbye. And neither had she.

The last few months had been a blur. The main practice in Helmston had sent various locums to take over at the surgery, and it had been heartbreaking to work alongside them every day, seeing them take her father's place. Sometimes she thought it would have been easier if she didn't work as the receptionist there, but then again it was a sort of comfort to go into his old consulting room and picture him sitting in his big leather chair, peering over his glasses at the computer screen in front of him. Sometimes, if she concentrated really hard, she was almost certain she could still smell his aftershave.

'Good day to you, Anna.' Maudie's round, rosy face was wreathed in smiles as Anna entered the shop. 'Big day for you today. You all packed?'

Anna nodded. 'Most of my stuff is already at Izzy's place. I just thought I'd buy in some essentials for the new doctor. You know, try to make the place a bit more welcoming.'

Maudie folded her arms and tilted her head to the side, eyeing her curiously. 'From Sheffield isn't he? Wonder what's made him head out here? He'll have a bit of a shock to the system I reckon. No supermarkets or cinemas or anything like that. I hope he knows what he's doing.'

'Probably another townie wanting a dream life in the country.' Anna grinned. 'You know what they're like. All excited about the fresh air and a new start, until reality kicks in and they realise how dismal our public transport is, and that there isn't a supermarket for miles. Let's just hope he's made of sterner stuff than most.'

They both laughed.

'Shame you had to get rid of your dad's chickens, though,' Maudie mused. 'You never know, this new chap might actually want to keep them.'

'Maybe so,' Anna said, 'but I couldn't take the risk. I had a buyer and I had to take the opportunity while it was there. If the new doctor wanted rid of them, I might not have had time to find somewhere else for them to go. You know, I only have a few weeks left here myself.'

Maudie sighed. 'You don't have to remind me. I will

miss you, love. I just can't imagine this place without you. Such a shame.' She brightened. 'Still, it's an exciting time for you. A new life down south with a new husband and home. And Lee's such a lovely boy, isn't he?'

Anna nodded. Lee had been her boyfriend since they were thirteen, but they'd been best friends since they were around six. They'd grown up together, and their parents had been friends, too. Everyone knew Lee and Anna were destined to be together. It was just the way things were.

Maybe, she thought wistfully, if he hadn't taken the job in Kent she wouldn't be experiencing these strange doubts that had attacked her with increasing frequency lately.

Maybe, if they were moving into a little cottage in the village, the way they'd always planned, she wouldn't be feeling so panicky, so lost.

Maybe she wouldn't be wondering if marrying Lee was the right thing to do, after all. There was no way of knowing, since Lee *had* taken the job in Kent, despite always promising to return to Yorkshire when he finished university. In five weeks' time, he would be coming back home, they'd be married in the nearest registry office, and then she'd be going back to Kent with him.

It wasn't what she'd imagined at all, and she knew

her father would have been dismayed. He'd always hoped to see them married in St Benedict's church in the village, surrounded by all their neighbours and friends. It was what she'd dreamed of, too. But then, her father wouldn't be there to walk her up the aisle, and it would never be the same without him. A registry office without any fuss seemed the best thing.

Besides, they didn't have time to plan anything grander now. Her father's replacement was on his way, Lee had started his new job, and the last few weeks had been a whirlwind of preparation and packing, as well as making sure things were in order at work, ready for her replacement to take over.

'So what's this new doctor like?' Maudie asked, as Anna picked up a basket and began to browse the shelves.

She shrugged. 'All I know is that he's got good references, and that he's on a three-month trial, during which time he'll rent our house. If he likes it, and he does okay, he'll be buying the place. That's the understanding we have anyway.'

'Fancy agreeing to that when he hasn't even seen the house for himself,' Maudie said, surprised.

'Well, he's seen photographs and details, and let's face it, there aren't many places for sale round here. Plus he needs to settle quickly apparently. He has a daughter.'

'A daughter? So there's a wife somewhere in the picture?'

Anna laughed. 'I have no idea. I just know there's a daughter. She could be the same age as me, for all I know. I know nothing else about them.'

'Well,' Maudie said with a sigh, as Anna handed her a basket containing basic provisions, a sponge cake, and a bunch of bright and cheerful spring flowers, 'we'll soon find out won't we?'

'We will,' Anna agreed, biting her lip pensively. The new arrivals would be at the house within a few hours, and then everything would change.

***

Connor Blake checked in his rear-view mirror and heaved a sigh of relief. His eight-year-old daughter, Gracie, was asleep. Well, that was a good thing he supposed, but he wished she'd fallen asleep a bit earlier. Like, maybe the moment they'd left Sheffield. He glanced back at her, and his expression softened. She looked so peaceful and sweet. Her brown, wavy hair tumbled to her shoulders, and long eyelashes swept her cheekbones as she slept. If only she looked that contented and relaxed when she was awake he thought sadly.

He looked at the Satnav. Not long now.

Bramblewick was less than ten minutes away, always supposing this contraption was accurate. He'd already gone on what appeared to him a totally unnecessary detour of the surrounding moorland. Plus, he'd found himself bouncing along an extremely narrow and bumpy lane, which had been quite alarming and thoroughly uncomfortable.

Gracie had definitely not liked that. She'd squealed and shut her eyes and covered her ears, and he'd wanted desperately to go back, but there was nowhere wide enough to turn around. It was only when he finally left the lane and entered the main road again that he'd glanced back and seen the sign, 'Public Bridlepath'. Well, that explained the frequent piles of manure, he thought, ruefully. Wretched Satnavs. Give him a good old road atlas any time.

He felt a fluttering sensation in his stomach as he wondered what lay ahead of him. He'd researched Bramblewick online, and it looked idyllic—stone cottages with red roofs beside a clear stream, an ancient church, a village green, and a traditional old pub, The Bay Horse. Deep in the Yorkshire Moors, surrounded by moorland, where sheep far outnumbered the human residents, it looked as if it could be the perfect place to start again.

On the other hand, he thought pensively, it could all go desperately wrong. Village life was completely new to him, but he suspected that people would want to know all about him. All about Gracie.

In a city it was easier to stay hidden, somehow, despite being in the midst of so many people. He hoped he'd made the right decision. At least there was a three-month trial period. If it was all too much for him, he could pack up any time, take Gracie and leave. His mother would happily put them up until they found a new home, and he was confident he could always get work somewhere. Sadly, GPs were in short supply.

The signpost loomed up ahead of him. Bramblewick.

Crossing the stone bridge over the stream, his gaze took in the village green, backed by a row of shops that began with a large and rather beautiful public house, and ended with a quaint little café.

His eyes widened as he noticed several sheep wandering happily outside the shops and meandering across the road in front of him. His gaze was drawn to the church — all cream and honey stone. A pretty churchyard, bright with the last of the daffodils lining neat gravel paths, was enclosed by a low hawthorn hedge, and he drove slowly past it, thinking he'd never seen a more picturesque little village.

Could they be happy here, after all? Was this the place where they would finally settle, make friends, build a new life? Would Gracie be okay here? Would she cope with this new way of living? It was the worry that plagued him day and night, and *What about Gracie?* was his constant recurring thought.

He heard her stirring and tried to quell the anxiety.

'Where are we, Daddy?'

He eyed her reflection in the mirror, giving her what he hoped was a reassuring smile.

'We're in Bramblewick, darling. I'm just looking for our house.'

She frowned, sitting up straight and staring out of the window, her forehead creased with worry.

He held his breath, but she said nothing. Slowly he exhaled and scanned the road, realising his new home overlooked the stream, and was quite stunningly pretty. Bemused, he noticed more sheep milling in the road, showing no signs that the sound of his car engine unsettled them. Drawing up in front of the house, he unclipped his seatbelt and made a conscious effort to relax his tense muscles. They were home.

He saw the curtains twitch at the front window, then the front door flew open, and a young woman, in jeans and a dark blue sweatshirt, hurried down the path, dark hair bobbing, a fixed smile on her face. He recognised that smile. It was the smile of someone who didn't really want to smile at all but was trying desperately not to show it. He used that smile himself, many times. He wondered what her problem was.

'Dr Blake?' She held out her hand as he stepped onto the pavement, and he shook it, noticing the conflict in her warm, blue eyes. 'I'm so pleased to meet you. I'm Anna Gray.'

Gray? Ah, it was beginning to make sense. He glanced up at the house and felt a pang of sympathy for her. This was her home—or had been. Now, with her father gone, she'd decided to move out. He felt a sudden guilt and wondered why. It was hardly his fault after all. But she wasn't that old—maybe in her late twenties—and for all he knew she hadn't had much choice in the matter. He wondered if she resented him. Wasn't she the receptionist at the surgery, too? That could make things awkward.

'Connor Blake,' he confirmed. A movement in the car caught his eye and he saw Gracie staring wide-eyed out of the window at the house. Anna smiled and waved to her, but Gracie made no response. He wasn't surprised by that, though Anna looked a little confused.

'Your daughter?' she enquired, as he opened the car door and coaxed Gracie out.

'Er, yes. Gracie, this is Anna Gray. Anna, this is my daughter, Gracie.'

Anna held out her hand. Connor held his breath, wondering how Gracie would react. Gracie was still looking at the house. She gave Anna a thumbs-up sign, and he breathed out again. All right, she didn't take the hand that had been offered to her, and she didn't smile, or respond verbally, but she'd reacted positively, which was something.

Anna dropped her hand and answered his daughter with a warm greeting. If she was flustered or puzzled, she didn't show it.

'Please come inside and I'll make us a cup of tea before I show you around. I expect you're ready for one after your journey. The heating's on, so it's warm and cosy in there.'

'Thank you. That's very kind of you.'

She turned and began to head back down the path towards the front door, and Connor almost made the mistake of putting his hand in Gracie's but remembered just in time that she didn't like being touched at the moment.

Instead he nodded at the front door, indicating that she should follow Anna which, thankfully, she did.

He decided he'd unload the car later. He needed a drink and to get his bearings first. He was already beginning to feel overwhelmed with doubt, and he'd only arrived in the village five minutes ago. He knew he had to overcome his anxieties. At some point he and Gracie had to put down roots and start again. Maybe Bramblewick would be the place they finally managed it.

Chapter 2

Anna glanced around the smallest bedroom, remembering when it had been her playroom.

'It's more of a box room, really,' she admitted. She had such happy memories of this house and showing these strangers around it had only brought home to her how much she was going to miss it. She hoped they appreciated what they had.

Dr Blake had nodded and made positive noises as he followed her through the house, but the little girl seemed completely uninterested.

'Perhaps this will be your room?' Anna queried, hoping to engage her somehow.

The girl didn't even look at her. Anna frowned. She wasn't exactly outgoing or friendly. Maybe she hadn't wanted to move to Bramblewick? She probably had loads of friends back in Sheffield and was going to miss them. It must be tough leaving everyone and everything familiar behind to start again when you were such a young child. It was tough enough as an adult. She couldn't imagine how she was going to settle in at the flat in Kent.

It was different for Lee. He'd been at university there for years, made new friends, built up a social life. She would know no one, and she'd have to look for a job, start her life all over again. She was dreading it. At least she had Lee, she supposed, much as this little one had her father. She wondered what had happened to her mother but didn't like to ask.

'I think Gracie will prefer the bigger back room,' Dr Blake said, glancing across at his daughter. There was a query in his voice, but Gracie didn't seem interested in confirming or denying his suspicions.

He hesitated a moment, then turned back to Anna.

'Well, that's the house explored. Thank you. It's just what I imagined.'

'So you think you'll like it here?' It was a stupid question, and she knew his answer before he gave it.

'Hard to tell right now. The house is just what we were looking for, but of course I haven't seen the village yet. Then I'll have to see how I get on in the job, and there's Gracie's school to consider...'

His voice trailed off and he rubbed his forehead, looking tired.

Anna smiled gently. 'Of course. Look, why don't I make you another cup of tea while you bring your suitcases in? Then I'll get off and leave you to it.'

'No, no.' His voice sounded sharp, and he shook his

head as if realising it. 'I'm sorry. I mean, please, sit down and let me make you one. I need to find my way around the kitchen after all.'

She frowned. His tone had changed, but he was clearly rattled about something.

'Well, if you're sure...'

'It must be hard for you,' he said, ten minutes later as he handed her a hot drink. 'Moving out of here, I mean. I understand you've lived here a long time?'

'All my life,' she confessed. 'Twenty-eight years. I can't imagine living anywhere else.' She looked around the living room, blinking away tears at the thought of leaving. She couldn't put it off much longer. Once she'd finished this tea she'd have no more excuses.

'Where will you go?'

She shrugged. 'I'm staying with an old schoolfriend for a few weeks. She only lives up the road, so I won't be far away. You do know I'm the receptionist at the surgery? At least, for now.'

'Yes, I knew that. Well, don't worry, your job's safe as far as I'm concerned.' He smiled at her, and she felt suddenly sorry for what she was about to tell him.

'I'm leaving in a few weeks. I'm moving to Kent. Don't worry though; they've already got my replacement lined up. She starts next week, training alongside me, so she should be ready to take over the reins when I go.'

'Kent?' He narrowed his eyes. 'That's a long way to go.'

'My boyfriend got a job there,' she began, then corrected herself. 'I mean, my fiancé. We're getting married in five weeks, so… I'll have to find myself a job, start over. So you see,' she finished, smiling back at him, 'I do understand how you must feel. Starting again in a whole new area, I mean. What made you decide to come to Bramblewick?'

He took another sip of his tea, as if considering how to reply. Her gaze followed his as he looked over at his daughter, who was sitting on the sofa, eyes closed, nodding gently now and then. Anna realised she was wearing earphones and was listening to something on the tablet she clutched in her hand.

'She loves her music,' he said softly.

Anna heard a sadness in his voice and wondered what lay behind it. 'I was just the same at her age,' she said. 'I used to drive my parents mad. They were always nagging me to turn my music off and pay attention to them.'

'I know the feeling.' He sighed. 'It's for her really—the move, I mean. She needed a settled home and a new start. It's been a tough couple of years.'

'I'm sorry to hear that.' She watched him for a moment, noting the shadows under his dark brown eyes, and the way he ran a hand through his hair as he considered his next words. He wasn't that old. Probably mid-thirties. Yet he seemed to have the weight of the world on his shoulders. 'I understand you've been a locum for quite a while.'

'Yes. Over a year.'

'I suppose there's more money and less responsibility,' she admitted. 'What made you decide to accept a full-time post?'

'Like I said, it's for Gracie mostly. It was easier, for a time, being a locum. I could fit in my hours around her, you see. But it's been a while now. I thought it best that she gets back into a settled routine. She needs a new home and a fresh start. We both do.' He nodded at the wall. 'Nice picture,' he said, referring to a painting on the wall above the fireplace.

Clearly he wanted to change the subject, so she played along with him. Besides, she'd always loved the picture. It was a print of *The Doctor* by Luke Fildes, and showed a concerned Victorian doctor, studying a poor, sick child. Watching on was the child's anxious father, his hand on the shoulder of his distraught wife. The doctor was a symbol of hope. The way he was looking at the child... As if he was willing him or her to recover.

When Anna was a little girl, she'd stared at that painting many times, imagining her father working in such conditions, having no concept of the National Health Service. As she got older, she'd realised that perhaps things had moved on a little since the painting was done, but it hadn't quelled her pride in what her father did for a living. The doctor in the painting was a hero, as much as her own father was to her. He would always be her hero.

'It's lovely isn't it?' She smiled. 'You're sure you don't mind me leaving my furniture here for now? I'll be taking it all with me when I go to Kent, but it seemed silly to move it twice, and the agent said you were happy to rent it fully furnished for the time being.'

'That's no problem. I've got my own things in storage until I decide for sure what I'm going to do. Like you, I didn't want to have to move them twice.'

'Well,' she put down her cup and stood, 'I suppose I'd better be going. It was lovely to meet you, and I'll see you on Monday at work.'

'You will.'

He held out his hand, rather formally, and she shook it solemnly.

'You know where the surgery is?'

'I'm sure I'll find it easily enough. It's not exactly a big village is it?' he said. 'You do know I'll be in late, that first morning? I should be there for around nine-thirty, then you can show me around before I start work.'

'Yes, I knew that. I expect you'll be taking Gracie to her new school.' Anna nodded towards the little girl, who was still listening to her music, oblivious to their conversation. 'How are you going to manage every day after that?'

'My mother is coming up tomorrow for a few weeks to help. Just until we get into a routine. She'll be taking Gracie to school initially. After that...' He looked worried for a moment. 'After that, I'm hoping she'll settle at the breakfast club, and I can drop her off there around eight each day. Then there's the after-school club until surgery closes. It was one of the deciding factors in the decision to move here, to be honest—the facilities available before and after school, and the quality of the school itself.'

'I see. Well, I'm sure she'll love it there. You're right. It's a great little school, and the breakfast club is very popular with working parents. I went there myself. The school, I mean, not the breakfast club. That's a fairly new development.'

He said nothing and she felt awkward again.

'Well,' she said, picking up her empty cup once more, 'I'll just put this in the sink, and I'll be off.'

He leapt up from his chair. 'Really, there's no need. I can put it away later.'

'Oh, it's no trouble,' she said, smiling at him. 'Let me take yours if you've finished.'

Pushing open the kitchen door, she carried the cups towards the sink and stopped dead. Sticking out of the waste bin were the stalks of the flowers that she'd bought and placed in a vase on the kitchen table.

He'd thrown away the flowers? Well, that was plain rude. If he hadn't wanted them, all he had to do was give them back to her. She heard him behind her and turned to face him, her expression stony.

'I'm sorry,' he said, clearly flustered. 'I—I can explain.'

'Can you?' She waited as he obviously searched for some plausible excuse.

'Hay fever,' he muttered eventually, then looked down at the floor.

'Hay fever. Right.' Anna headed into the hallway. 'Thanks for the tea. Say goodbye to your daughter for me, and I'll see you on Monday.'

'Anna!' She turned to see him staring at her, a pale pink flush across his high cheekbones.

'Yes?'

'I'm sorry.' He'd already said that once and repeating the apology didn't make her feel any better. She nodded and left the house, thinking that maybe it was a good thing she wouldn't be around for much longer. The new doctor and his daughter were definitely odd. She'd be better off out of it.

***

Rose Cottage was just past the pub on the main road through the village and was much smaller than her own home. Her *old* home, Anna corrected herself, as she headed towards the cottage, passing the café, Maudie's shop, the tiny post office and gift shop, the butcher's, and The Bay Horse, finally reaching what was to be her home for the next month, thanks to the generosity of her old schoolfriend, Izzy.

It might be small but it was pretty. Like the house she'd just left behind her, it had oak beams and a wood burning stove, and Izzy had decorated it in a pretty, vintage style that made it cosy and welcoming. It would be no hardship living there for a few weeks, even if the spare bedroom was barely big enough to accommodate a single bed and a wardrobe.

Izzy was in the kitchen, slicing leeks on a chunky, wooden chopping board. She smiled brightly at Anna as she entered the room, her green eyes showing sympathy. 'All done? How was it?'

'Difficult,' Anna admitted. 'I can't believe I've actually left there for the last time. I feel like crying.'

Izzy put down the knife and gave her a hug. 'I'm sorry, Anna. I know how difficult this must be for you. Hey, I'm making chicken casserole, followed by apple pie and custard. Always cheers you up, if I remember correctly, and it will warm you up too.'

Anna laughed. 'You know me so well,' she

confirmed. 'Anything I can do to help?'

'Nope. All under control. Have you finished unpacking?' She patted Anna's arm as her friend shook her head. 'Well, then, go and get that sorted. I'll give you a shout when it's ready.'

Anna's clothes barely fitted into the wardrobe in the compact bedroom, but she just about managed to squeeze everything in. Sinking onto the single bed, she glanced out of the window, smiling at two children playing in the fields behind the house, wondering why they didn't appear to feel the cold. The April air outside was sharp, yet they didn't seem to notice.

She thought about Gracie Blake. She was a strange child, no doubt about it. It was understandable if she was feeling sad at leaving her old home and friends behind, but even so. She wondered again about the little girl's mother. Connor hadn't been wearing a wedding ring, not that that proved anything. Lots of married men didn't wear them. Which reminded her...

Digging in her bag, she retrieved her mobile phone and called Lee. It was a minute or so before he answered her, and he sounded breathless.

'Sorry, have I interrupted you?' she enquired.

'No, of course not. Well, I was just getting ready to go out,' he admitted.

'Oh? And where are you disappearing off to?' she teased. 'I hope you're behaving yourself down there.'

'Of course I am,' he replied, sounding indignant. 'Some of the blokes from work invited me out, that's all. They're going to introduce me to a new place—one of their favourite pubs, apparently. It will make a change from The Dog and Duck at any rate. You don't mind do you? I'm just trying to build a social life, and it will benefit us both in the long run.'

'Of course I don't mind,' she said, meaning it.

'Hey, how did it go?' he said suddenly. 'The new doctor arrived today didn't he? What's he like?'

She thought about the flowers, stuffed unceremoniously in the bin.

'He's okay,' she said. 'Bit quiet, but I expect I'll get used to him.' Wistfully she realised that she wouldn't get the chance. She wouldn't be around long enough.

'I'm sorry. It must have been horrible for you, leaving the house behind.' His tone was sympathetic, and she gripped the phone, wishing he was there with her. She could use a hug from her best friend. 'How are you settling in at Izzy's?'

'Only just got here,' she admitted. 'She's just making me something to eat and then I suspect it will be a girly night in, watching some chick flick and scoffing chocolate.'

'Good for you.' He was quiet for a moment, then said, 'Well, anyway, I've got to go, Anna. I'm running a bit late as it is. You take care of yourself, and I'll speak to you tomorrow, okay?'

'Okay. Have a good night,' she said.

'Love you.'

'Love you too,' she replied automatically, and ended the call.

'All done?' Izzy was just putting the plates on the table when Anna re-entered the kitchen. 'Did you manage to fit everything in? If not I may be able to make space in my room. I can always put some of my stuff in a suitcase under the bed for now.'

'No, there's no need. I managed. Luckily, I've never been one for buying a lot of clothes,' Anna reminded her, knowing that her friend had never understood that being a bit of a fashion slave.

They sat at the table and Anna realised suddenly how hungry she was.

'This looks delicious,' she said, enthusiastically spooning mashed potatoes onto her plate.

'Good.' Izzy grinned at her. 'Enjoy, because it's your turn to cook tomorrow.'

They tucked in, barely making conversation as they hungrily devoured the meal. Eventually, Anna put down her knife and fork and leaned back in her chair.

'I'm done,' she admitted. 'I'm afraid that apple pie will have to wait a while.'

'I know what you mean.' Izzy picked up her glass of wine and took a sip. 'That was gorgeous if I do say so myself. So are you up for a Bridget Jones DVD later?'

Anna laughed. 'I knew it! I was just saying to Lee that no doubt we'd be watching a chick flick tonight.'

'Oh, you've spoken to Lee today? I knew he'd call to see how you got on. How is he?'

'He was about to go out, actually,' Anna said. 'And I called him. Not that it matters.'

'Oh.' Izzy took another sip of wine, then returned her glass to the table. 'Well, anyway, I'm sure he'll behave himself.'

Anna raised an eyebrow. 'What an odd thing to say! Of course he'll behave himself.'

'Don't you ever worry?' Izzy sounded genuinely curious. 'I mean, with him being down there all by himself. No one to keep an eye on him. Don't you ever get anxious that he'll, you know, meet someone else?'

'Lee? Seriously?' Anna shrugged. 'No I don't. He wouldn't do that. He's as reliable as they come. Besides, he's my best friend. He would never do anything to hurt me.'

Izzy sighed. 'It must be lovely to be in such a solid relationship. Wish I could find someone like Lee.'

Anna laughed. 'Someone like Lee would drive you mad. He's far too dull for you. You want someone flashier and more unpredictable. Lee would bore you to tears.'

'Hmm. Maybe once. But there's a lot to be said for

predictable if you ask me. I haven't exactly been lucky in love, have I? And there's not an awful lot of choice round here, is there? Talking of which, go on, tell me. What's this new doctor like?'

'Quiet. A bit strained and tired looking to be honest.' She remembered the dark shadows under his eyes, and the tension in his mouth. She wondered what was keeping him awake at night.

'But what does he look like? Is he—you know—a bit of a babe? Or am I to be disappointed, yet again?'

Anna thought about it. 'Well, yes, I suppose he is rather attractive,' she admitted eventually. 'But I've got a feeling he comes with baggage.'

'You mean his daughter?'

Anna looked at her in surprise. 'You know about his daughter? Oh well, I suppose you would. You never mentioned though!'

Izzy was a teacher at the village primary school, so it was inevitable that she'd have been expecting the new arrival. It wasn't a big school after all, and there weren't that many pupils.

Izzy ran her finger around the rim of her glass, looking thoughtful. 'Gracie, isn't it? Yes, she's not in my class, but...'

Her voice trailed off and Anna eyed her warily.

'But what?'

'Oh, nothing. So, he's good looking, eh? Well, I may

just suddenly come down with a mysterious virus in the next few days. Don't be surprised to find me in the surgery waiting room one morning.'

Anna laughed. 'You're terrible. Somehow I get the impression he's not looking for love. Anyway, for all we know there's a wife on the scene.'

Izzy took a gulp of wine, and Anna watched her curiously. There was something Izzy wasn't telling her, she was sure. But then again, it was none of her business. What did it matter anyway? She'd be gone soon. Only five weeks to her big day and then...

'Good grief!' She sat up straight, her eyes wide.

'What is it?'

'I still haven't got anything to wear for the wedding! Can't believe I haven't even looked yet.'

'Neither can I. Honestly, Anna, what kind of a bride shows no interest in organising her own wedding? Only a few weeks to go and you've done nothing. Well, we'll have to rectify that,' Izzy said firmly. 'Let's look online, see if we spot anything you like. Then,' she added, 'we'll put that film on, and I'll fetch another bottle of wine from the fridge. But first—'

'First?' Anna thought that sounded like quite enough.

'First,' said Izzy, with a gleam in her eye, 'let's make a start on that apple pie!'

Chapter 3

Connor, despite his determination not to show it, couldn't hide his relief when he opened the front door to find his mother standing there, small suitcase in hand.

She beamed at him, and he enfolded her in a hug.

'You're early! I wasn't expecting you until this afternoon. Why didn't you call me from the station?'

'I got a taxi,' she said, indicating the gleaming silver car that was driving back over the little stone bridge.

'A taxi! It must have cost a fortune from the station.' He took the case from her hand. 'Why on earth didn't you ring me? You know I said I'd collect you.'

She tutted and pushed past him, looking around her as she walked down the hallway. 'I think you've done enough driving with the journey up here yesterday. Besides, I didn't want to disturb Gracie unnecessarily.' She eyed him steadily. 'How is she? Where is she?'

He sighed. 'Where do you think?'

'Not *Phantom of the Opera* again?' She shook her head. 'Obsessed she is. Absolutely obsessed. How did it go last night? Did she settle?'

He showed her into the kitchen, motioning to her to sit down at the table while he refilled the kettle.

'You look tired out,' she murmured. 'I guess that's my answer.'

'She didn't like the wallpaper in her bedroom,' he explained, 'so we had to move all her things into a smaller room across the landing. It took ages, and then she wouldn't settle until I'd swapped the curtains. And she's started with the light switches again.'

'Oh no.' Mrs Blake pulled out a chair and put her head in her hands. 'I thought we'd got past that one. Used to drive me insane. Flick, flick, flick. Light on, light off, light on, light off. She'll be blowing the bulb again. Is it every room or just her bedroom?'

'Just her bedroom, thank goodness,' he said, pouring hot water over teabags. 'Oh, and all doors must be shut. Every door, every drawer in the house. She checked them repeatedly last night.'

'No wonder you look so tired,' she said, her voice rich with sympathy.

He handed her a mug of tea and sat beside her.

'Do you think I've done the right thing, Mum? Bringing her here, away from her school, from everything that's familiar to her?'

'She didn't exactly have any friends to leave, did she?' she pointed out gently. 'And that school was rubbish. Absolutely clueless. Besides, that house had nothing but bad memories, and you wanted a full-time job again, so why not here? It seems to be a very pretty village, from what I could see as we drove over the bridge, and this house is lovely.'

'But it is a village,' he reminded her. 'And you know what villages are like. What if they all want to know about her? What if they don't take to her?'

'You're going to have the same problems wherever you go,' she said, her eyes soft with sadness. 'I'm sorry to have to say it, but you know it's true. So why not settle here? It's as good as anywhere else, and who knows, with it being a smaller school she might get the attention she needs. Let's face it, it couldn't be any worse, could it?'

The unspoken acknowledgment hung in the air between them. Connor cradled the mug of tea, knowing what she said was true. He'd spoken to the headmistress at Bramblewick Primary School, and she'd assured him they would be able to cope with Gracie.

'What we don't know now, we'll learn soon enough,' she'd said cheerfully. 'We firmly believe that every child deserves the best education, and we do all we can to ensure they get the chances they deserve. Gracie will be no exception. Rest assured, Dr Blake, we'll do our very best for her.'

Her positivity and encouragement had been the deciding factor in the end. His mother was right. Things couldn't be any worse for Gracie than they had been at her old school. The teachers there hadn't understood and showed no interest in trying to find out. He longed for her to feel safe, included, wanted. Maybe in this village she'd get the chances she deserved.

'Have you been for a look around the place yet?' His mother's voice broke through his thoughts, bringing him back to the present.

He shook his head. 'Not yet. It was hectic yesterday. Unpacking. Trying to settle her. You know.'

'I know,' she nodded. 'So, you've not met anyone? None of the neighbours?'

'Not the neighbours, no,' he said hesitantly. 'I did meet one person. The woman who used to live here. You know, the doctor's daughter.'

'Oh, yes. Poor mite. Not long lost her father, has she? How was she?'

He thought about the flowers, stuffed in the bin, and felt his face start to burn with shame. It had been a kind gesture and look what he'd done to repay it. He could still see the stunned expression on her face, quickly replaced with a look of disgust.

'She seems nice enough,' he said finally. 'She's the receptionist at the surgery, so I'll be seeing her quite a bit over the next few weeks.'

Her face took on a familiar, eager look. 'Really? How old is she? Is she pretty?'

He sighed. 'She's leaving in a few weeks, Mum. Off to live in Kent with her new husband.'

'Oh.' The disappointment was written all over her face, and he squeezed her hand.

'You have to stop hoping to fix me up, you know,' he told her. 'Let's be honest. It's never going to happen.'

'Of course it will happen. You can't give up on all women, just because of the way Tina behaved. Not everyone's so shallow and—'

'Mum, don't.' He shook his head, not wanting to go over it all again. 'Tina isn't shallow. She just—she just couldn't cope. I doubt very much that any other woman will be able to deal with Gracie if her own mother couldn't, so there's no point in even looking. Besides,' he added wearily, 'I haven't got the energy to even think about starting a relationship with someone else. My focus is on Gracie and making her happy, giving her the best life I can possibly give her. That's enough for me.'

'Well, it shouldn't be,' she protested. 'You're only thirty-five, for goodness sake. You have such a lot to offer, and besides, you deserve someone to love you.'

'Gracie loves me, in her own way,' he said. 'And of course,' he added, his face breaking into a grin, 'I've always got you, haven't I?'

She laughed and nudged him. 'Oh, you've always got me, love,' she acknowledged. 'Even so,' she added, her smile fading again, 'I wish... Oh well, whatever you say. Time to say hello to my granddaughter, though lord knows, I shouldn't think for a moment that she'll thank me for interrupting her film.'

***

Anna wasn't happy. She had an awful feeling she'd been landed with a dud in Beverley, the woman the practice manager had hired to take her place in less than a month's time. She claimed to have experience working in other surgeries, but she didn't seem to have a clue what Anna was talking about as she showed her round, explaining the computer system and going over the appointments with her.

'You have worked as a receptionist before?' she queried, thinking she may as well check, just to be on the safe side.

'Oh, yes,' Beverley said airily, 'and I have to say, after working in such a big health centre, this little place seems a doddle.'

That got Anna's back up straight away. A doddle! Well, they'd soon see how much of a doddle Beverley thought it was at the end of her first week, she thought indignantly. It was a common misconception at the main practice in town that the branch surgery at Bramblewick was so small that it needed hardly any time or attention. They were ignored half the time, and more-or-less left to deal with any problems themselves, since the large parent building with its eight doctors, six nurses, and a whole team of receptionists and secretaries, demanded the lion's share of both funds and focus. After all, a small surgery on the outskirts of a village with one doctor, one receptionist, and twice-weekly sessions with a nurse was hardly worth bothering with, was it? Evidently not, she thought bitterly. And clearly, not much time or effort had gone into making sure the new receptionist was suitable for the job, which was deeply worrying, given she herself would be leaving shortly and the new doctor hadn't a clue what went on there.

Talking of the new doctor, Anna frowned as she noticed the time on the corner of the computer screen. It was almost ten to ten. He'd said he would be there for half past nine. Good job his surgery didn't start until the afternoon, she thought, although it was still annoying. She had loads to go over with him before then, and the locum would be wanting a cup of tea soon, and she still had to deal with this incompetent woman who clearly had little idea what was expected of her. Great.

Coming out of the consulting room at just gone ten, having delivered a drink to the locum, Anna entered the tiny office behind the reception to find Connor Blake standing awkwardly by her desk. Beverley, who was supposed to be familiarising herself with the repeat prescription electronic system, was gazing up at him in clear admiration. Anna felt her hackles rising.

'You made it then?' she said, her voice sounding sharper than she'd intended. She'd just about had enough of today already, and his lack of punctuality had only wound her up even further.

He straightened, his stare piercing through her, making her wish she'd spoken a little less harshly. He was, strictly speaking, her boss, after all.

'I did. I apologise for my lateness, but it couldn't be helped. Shall we make a start?'

'Er, yes. I'll show you to your consulting room first,' she said, her cheeks feeling hot.

Damn! She was blushing. She glared as Beverley shot her a smug look.

'Beverley, put the kettle on for Dr Blake, please,' she instructed. 'Will you follow me?' she added, turning back to Connor.

He nodded, saying nothing, and she headed down the corridor to his room. Well, that was a great start, she thought dismally. Thank goodness she wouldn't have to put up with the two of them for much longer.

***

'I don't quite understand this,' Connor said, peering out into the waiting room.

Anna glanced up from scanning a report onto a patient's computer file and raised an eyebrow. 'Don't understand what?'

Afternoon surgery wasn't due to start for another hour, and she thought she'd already gone over everything he needed to know for now. The finer details could wait. He had a lot of patients to get through, and if a locum could manage it without any instructions, she was sure he could manage too.

She wasn't feeling kindly disposed towards him, at that moment, and her patience had been stretched to the limit already by Beverley's clear bewilderment. No doubt about it. She'd duped the practice manager. If she had as much experience of reception work as she claimed to have, she was either a very good actress or had the memory of a goldfish.

Connor nodded at the packed waiting room. 'This,' he said again.

Anna followed his gaze. The seats were all full and, in spite of herself, she smiled as she recognised all the villagers who sat, happily chatting to each other as they waited. It was par for the course most afternoons, especially if the weather was good, but she could well imagine how it appeared to a stranger.

'I mean,' Connor continued, sounding baffled, 'according to the appointment screen, I'm seeing around eighteen patients this afternoon, right?'

She nodded, knowing what was coming. 'Well, even if they've all come at once, and I highly doubt that they would hang around for up to three hours to see me, that doesn't explain why there are around thirty people sitting out there now, especially a whole hour before surgery. Is there something else going on here? A clinic I'm not aware of perhaps?'

Beverley batted her eyelashes at him. 'I reckon they've all come to see what you look like,' she said coyly.

'I shouldn't think so, not for a minute.'

Anna peered at him. Was he blushing? She found she was grinning and tried to straighten her face.

'I think she's probably right,' she admitted. 'Word spreads quickly around here, and they all want to know what the new doctor is like. Although, you'll get used to this. Quite often, people come to sit in here just to have a catch up. It's sort of an unofficial meeting place most afternoons.'

'You're joking, right?' He looked appalled, and she shook her head.

'I'm not joking. They don't do any harm.'

He opened his mouth to speak but the telephone silenced him.

Beverley picked up the receiver. 'Good afternoon, Bramblewick Surgery. Beverley speaking, can I help?'

Her face screwed up in concentration as she listened to whoever was on the other end of the phone, as Anna hovered, ready to offer advice if necessary.

Beverley pressed the mute button. 'Is there a visit booked for a Mrs Brown at Fleece Cottage?'

Anna knew the answer to that but wasn't about to give it to her.

'Check on the patient's record,' she reminded her. 'Click on the visits link in the admin tab.'

Beverley tutted. 'Oh, yeah.'

She typed the patient's name and clicked her mouse a couple of times. 'Yeah, there is. You're supposed to be visiting her before surgery,' she told Connor.

'Okay, so is there a problem?' Anna asked.

Beverley unmuted the phone and said, 'Yes, Dr Blake will be there in two shakes of a lamb's tail. Everything okay?'

Anna rolled her eyes and waited as Beverley listened again. 'Oh, right. Yeah, okay. I'll pass the message on. No, no worries. I can't say I blame you. Okay. See you later.'

'What is it?' Connor demanded before Anna got the chance.

'Mrs Brown said, can you call at the butcher's and grab her a pound of beef sausages?'

Connor looked incredulous. 'Pardon?'

Anna cleared her throat. 'Oh, yes, about that. Some of the patients—that is, some of the older patients—well, they sort of expect that the doctor will, er, you know, pop in to the shops and bring them in some provisions. It's kind of a tradition.'

'It's a ridiculous tradition!' Connor spluttered. 'Who on earth thought of that?'

Anna bridled. 'My father actually.'

His face reddened. 'Oh, yes, of course. Well, I can appreciate that he'd been here a long time, but really, I can't go calling into shops and buying stuff for patients. I have visits to get through and then surgery. It's just not done.'

'Says who?' she demanded. 'Just because you've never done it before doesn't make it wrong. The villagers really appreciated my dad's help, and he was always happy to take them a few things in, because he cared about them, and about their welfare. It won't take five minutes to call at the butcher's, and you won't have to worry about paying for anything because most of us have an account there. We just settle up at the weekends.'

'You can't let her down,' Beverley said, with a sly grin. 'She really needs those sausages. She's sick of chops.'

'For heaven's sake!' Connor looked from one to the other. 'This is madness. I'm not going to the shop for Mrs Brown, or anyone else for that matter.'

'But you have to,' protested Anna. 'Otherwise she may have nothing to eat for her tea tonight. Do you want that on your conscience?'

They glared at each other, then Connor slammed his hand on the table.

'Fine. I'll go to the wretched shop. Get me the patient's notes, will you please?' he said to Beverley. 'I'd better go early since I have a shopping list to get through.'

'Er, there may be more than one,' Anna admitted. 'You're seeing Mr Henley today, too, and he usually wants a loaf. Plus, Maudie does a really nice bacon quiche and he's very partial to that as a treat on visit days.'

Connor's eyes were like saucers. Muttering to himself, he stormed out of the office, back to his consulting room.

Beverley tutted and turned back to her computer. 'That went down well,' she drawled.

Anna tutted. 'Just print off the notes, please,' she said. She really didn't trust herself to say anything else.

Chapter 4

It felt strange, upon leaving work at six, to head towards Rose Cottage rather than Chestnut House. Trying not to brood upon it, Anna hitched the strap of her bag higher onto her shoulder and stuck her hands in her pockets. It was a chilly evening in early April, and far too cold to dawdle, while she brooded upon her sudden homesickness, especially on top of the terrible day she'd had.

At least she'd got her wedding outfit sorted, although Izzy didn't really approve. It wasn't that she didn't like the dress, she'd assured Anna. It was a perfectly pleasant, rather pretty day dress. The problem was it was just that. A day dress, not a wedding dress.

'It's just a registry office wedding,' Anna had reminded her, but Izzy wasn't having any of it.

'It's still your wedding,' she'd pointed out. 'Surely you want something a bit special? You could be wearing this for a garden party or even lunch at The Bay Horse.'

'It will do,' Anna said firmly. 'No point spending a

lot of money on such a small event. It would have been different if I was getting married at St Benedict's with most of the village attending, but I'm not, and they're not. It's a simple little event in town. No need to fuss.'

Izzy sighed. 'It's such a shame. You always wanted your wedding to be in the church where your parents got married. Are you sure you're doing the right thing?'

Anna was startled at the question. 'By marrying Lee?'

Izzy laughed. 'Of course not by marrying Lee. That's a given. I mean the wedding. Couldn't you put it off a while, give yourself more time to organise a proper do? I'm happy for you to stay here as long as you want, and I'm sure Lee would understand.'

Anna shook her head. 'No. I'm not postponing it. It has to be done, so we may as well get it over with.'

'What a way to look at it!' her friend had exclaimed.

'Okay, I admit it doesn't sound very romantic,' Anna admitted. 'But with Dad gone, I just can't face it. It doesn't seem right, somehow, to go ahead with my dream wedding when he's not here.'

Izzy put her arm around her. 'I suppose you're right. Anyway, it's the marriage that matters, not the wedding, and that will be perfect, right?'

'Well, maybe not perfect,' Anna said. 'No such thing as the perfect marriage after all.'

'As good as,' Izzy said, confidently. 'You and Lee are so right together. If anyone can be happy, it's you two.'

As Anna headed past The Bay Horse, she wondered why she didn't share Izzy's confidence. After all, everyone agreed that she and Lee made the perfect couple, and they'd barely had a cross word in all the years they'd been together. He was her best friend, and she loved him. So why did she feel so uncertain about their future?

Mentally shaking her head she trudged up the path towards Rose Cottage. She was just dreading leaving the village, that was all. It was all to do with her new life in Kent. Nothing to do with Lee, or their relationship.

'Oh, that smells gorgeous!' Sniffing eagerly, she threw down the bag and sank onto a chair in the kitchen, smiling at Izzy, resplendent in new pyjamas, as she busily stirred something in a pan.

'Chilli con carne,' Izzy said. 'My favourite. I don't tend to bother making it much, living on my own, but now there are two of us I have an excuse. How did it go today? New doctor, new receptionist. Bet you had your hands full, guiding them both through it all.'

Anna gave her a wry look. 'You have no idea.'

'Ooh. So, go on, spill the beans.'

'I will, over dinner. Have I got time to shower and change first? I feel slightly overdressed in this uniform, given your own casual attire.'

'Sure, go ahead. Fifteen minutes only mind.'

Newly showered and wearing clean pyjamas, Anna headed downstairs and poured two glasses of wine, as Izzy dished out the chilli con carne and rice.

'Oh, my goodness, that's just what I needed,' she pronounced a short time later, as she put down her spoon and stared regretfully at the empty plate. 'I could eat that all over again.'

'None left,' Izzy admitted. 'We've scoffed the lot. Hard day at work for me, how about you?'

'You could say that.' Anna stood and began to load the dishwasher. 'Let's get this cleared away and then we can drink our wine in the living room and tell each other our tales of woe.'

Ten minutes later they were curled up on the sofa, sipping wine and beginning to relax.

'So go on,' Izzy urged. 'How did the newbies settle in?'

Anna took a deep breath. 'Well, for starters, Beverley is absolutely awful. I mean, if she was completely new to the job I'd understand it, and I'd be far more patient. But she claims to have vast experience as a GP's receptionist, and, according to her CV, she should be able to handle the work with ease. In fact, she reckoned our place is a doddle compared to her old surgery.'

'But?'

'But she was completely out of her depth. If she

really did work at a surgery before, I can only assume that she was the worst receptionist ever and didn't absorb a single thing. I suspect the practice manager hasn't bothered to read the references. After all, it's only the Bramblewick Branch Surgery. Not the main Castle Street Practice. We're barely on their radar to be honest.'

'Oh dear. And what about Doctor Dreamboat?'

Anna stared at her. 'Who?'

'Don't deny it!' Izzy grinned. 'You're not blind. I couldn't believe it when I saw him this morning. He's gorgeous! You kept that quiet, didn't you?'

'He's all right,' Anna muttered, wondering why she could feel her skin heating up. 'But he's not going to fit in in this village if he doesn't loosen up a bit.'

'Meaning?'

'Meaning he was grumpy, uncooperative, and pretty scathing about our ways. He was really annoyed about having to call at the butcher's to pick up some shopping for Mrs Brown, for a start.'

Izzy spluttered into her wine glass. 'Well, come on. It's hardly usual for a doctor to do a patient's shopping is it?'

'In Bramblewick it is,' Anna said firmly. 'And if he wants to stay here he's going to have to make more of an effort to do things our way. And he didn't approve of the way the pensioners turned up to have a gossip to each other in the waiting room. As if it matters! They're not hurting anyone are they?'

'Well, no,' Izzy said cautiously, 'but it's not the norm. I know people who have been really astonished when they moved here and saw how things were done. It's not like any other surgery they've ever been to, apparently.'

'Dad didn't want it to be like any other surgery,' Anna pointed out. 'He wanted everyone to feel so welcome and relaxed that they weren't afraid to come to him if they felt unwell. He said too many people had a dread of visiting the doctor and put off going until it was too late. He was determined that, in our village, people would never be afraid to go and see him. Besides, they're all our friends, our neighbours. They're always welcome. And as for the shopping, why shouldn't we help them? It wasn't out of his way for goodness sake. A lot of fuss just because Mrs Brown wanted sausages instead of pork chops.'

Izzy giggled. 'Honestly, Anna, what's normal to you really sounds weird to other people. Don't be too hard on him, eh?'

'I probably wouldn't have been,' she admitted, 'if Beverley hadn't already wound me up. And then he had the cheek to arrive late! I mean, we'd already agreed he could come in at half past nine instead of nine, but in the end it was gone ten before he bothered to turn up.'

'Ah. Well.' Izzy stared into her wine glass, as if unsure whether to continue with that particular line of conversation or not.

'Do you know something I don't?' Anna demanded.

'Just that, well, Gracie didn't exactly settle easily this morning.'

'Oh. Well, that's a shame,' Anna conceded. 'Even so, surely it didn't take an hour to calm her down? Besides, her grandmother was supposed to be with her, so did he really have to stay so long?'

There was a moment's silence as Izzy contemplated her wine.

'Izzy?'

Izzy shifted, tucking a strand of her fair hair behind her ear, then taking a sip of wine. 'Okay,' she said eventually. 'You're probably going to hear about it anyway, because there were plenty of witnesses and this is a small village.'

'Hear about what?' Anna was puzzled. 'What happened?'

'Gracie—well, she kind of flipped out. I mean, she screamed and protested all the way to school. Honestly, we could hear her from inside the building. She was in a real state. It took Dr Blake and her grandmother ages to coax her into the school and calming her down was a real job.'

'You're kidding?'

'No. I felt really sorry for the doctor and his mum. They looked so upset and exhausted. It can't be easy for them, trying to deal with her.'

Anna frowned. 'What do you mean? What's wrong with her? Because I can tell from your face that she's not just a naughty child.'

'She's not,' Izzy said. 'Thing is, Anna, she's on the autism spectrum. I think they're all really struggling.'

Anna wasn't sure how to respond to that. She didn't know an awful lot about autism, but she knew enough to share her friend's concern. Poor Dr Blake. And she'd been so horrible to him at the surgery too.

'Funny thing is,' Izzy continued, 'when she actually settled down and stopped shouting and throwing herself around, she did really well. I mean, she's pretty intelligent, and she certainly knew how to do the work Ash Uttridge set her. By the end of the day she seemed really happy and settled. It's all very odd. Such a shame.' She yawned. 'Can't believe how tired I am, and it's not even eight. Shall we put the television on? Something funny to wake us up and make us laugh.'

'Yes, sure. Go for it,' Anna said, as Izzy reached for the remote. 'But what about tomorrow? Do you think they'll have the same problem all over again?'

'Who knows?' Izzy shook her head. 'I have to say, I'm quite glad she's in Ash's class rather than mine. I'm not sure I'd be up to it, but Ash has had some experience with autistic children in a previous job. It seems poor Gracie didn't have much luck at her last school. The reports from there are deeply unsympathetic and display a poor knowledge and understanding of the condition. Hopefully, Ash will be able to get through to her.'

'Gosh, I hope so,' Anna murmured. 'For all their sakes.'

Izzy turned on the television. 'Ooh, a rerun of *Blackadder*. Absolutely love that show. Is that okay with you?'

'What? Oh yes, yes fine.' Anna was barely listening. She was remembering the dark shadows under Connor Blake's eyes, and the weary look in his face. She was remembering, too, the little girl sitting hunched on the sofa, eyes closed, shutting out the world as she listened to her music. Suddenly, it didn't matter what was on the television because she couldn't see the screen anyway. Her eyes were too blurry with tears.

***

Connor felt as if he'd had his guts ripped out as he walked out of the school gates. It had taken ages to get Gracie into the school and now she was sobbing in the headmistress's room. He hadn't wanted to leave her and wouldn't have done if his mother hadn't assured him that she could manage, and that he wasn't to worry.

'Get yourself off to work,' she said, practically pushing him out of the door as the headmistress nodded sympathetically at him. 'We can cope and, besides, she'll calm down within half an hour, just as she did yesterday. We'll take her to the classroom, get her involved in some work, and she'll be a different girl. You know this, Connor. Go on, get to the surgery. They'll be wondering where you are.'

He knew, deep down, that she was right, but it didn't stop him feeling as if he'd betrayed Gracie as he walked away. He wondered what was going to happen when his mother was ready to go home. He could only pray that whoever ran the breakfast club would be patient and understanding and cooperate with Gracie's teacher to get her safely into the classroom.

Either that, or he'd have to throw himself on the mercy of his practice manager—beg to start surgery half an hour or so later than usual.

He glanced at his watch. He was already running late. Surgery was due to start in less than five minutes and he should be in his consulting room now, logging on, preparing for the day.

He wouldn't have time to make himself a cup of coffee, and he hadn't even grabbed any breakfast. His stomach had been in knots that morning, and no amount of pleading from his mother could persuade him to try anything—not even a slice of toast.

He regretted that decision now. He had a long morning ahead of him. On top of everything else, he could picture Anna's disapproving face when he arrived for work. She'd made it quite plain the previous day that she disapproved of his lack of punctuality. He supposed he had a lot to live up to in her eyes, what with her father being so perfect.

In the event she was nowhere to be seen when he walked into the office. Beverley was on the phone, and she rolled her eyes, as if to indicate that she had little sympathy for whoever she was talking to, then gave him a cheery thumbs-up.

He wasn't entirely convinced that she was cut out for the job and wondered what it would be like when she was his sole receptionist. Anna may be a little judgemental, but at least she knew what she was doing. Beverley didn't appear to have a clue.

As she put down the receiver she tutted at him, shaking her head in an exaggerated fashion. 'Late again, Dr Blake. I dunno. You've made the nasty lady very cross.'

He groaned inwardly. 'What did she say?'

Beverley laughed. 'Nothing. I'm kidding. Chill your beans.'

Chill your beans! She wasn't the most professional person he'd ever encountered, that was for sure. Still, at least she wasn't looking pointedly at the clock and tapping her foot. That was something.

'Where is Anna?'

'Dunno.' Beverley frowned. 'Maybe gone to the loo or something.'

'Oh. Right.' Flummoxed, he headed to the consulting room. Unlocking the door, he hurried in and switched on his computer, opening the vertical blind at the window as he waited for it to start up.

A knock on the door startled him. Surely the first patient hadn't been ushered in already? He hadn't buzzed them through but, knowing Beverley, she wouldn't wait for him to do so.

'Come in.'

The door opened slowly, and Anna came in, a smile on her face and a mug in one hand, a plate of biscuits balanced on top of it. He stared at her, astonished. It was the last thing he'd expected.

'Good morning, Dr Blake.'

He swallowed, then nodded. 'Good morning, Anna. Please, call me Connor.'

He'd already asked her twice, but she seemed unable to bring herself to do so. He was quite surprised when she set down the mug and plate on his desk and stepped back, saying, 'Sorry. Good morning, Connor. Did Gracie get off to school okay?'

His eyes narrowed. What did she know about

Gracie's antics at school? 'She, er, did. I'm sorry I'm a little late but—'

'Oh, honestly, it really doesn't matter.' Her eyes were warm as she looked at him. She had dark blue eyes, he noticed, and rather long eyelashes. 'You'll soon catch up.'

'I—I expect I will, yes. Thanks for the coffee and biscuits. I haven't had breakfast, so they're very welcome.'

She had a lovely complexion. Creamy skin, but with roses in her cheeks, and a slight dusting of freckles across her nose. She looked totally different when she smiled. He remembered how she'd smiled as she'd welcomed them to Chestnut House, and how kind she'd been.

Until she'd found the flowers in the bin, that was. He still felt dreadful about that. It was sheer panic. How could he explain that just the smell of them could freak Gracie out? There were certain flowers she liked, but others drove her mad. It wasn't Anna's fault that she'd chosen ones Gracie wouldn't tolerate.

Anna nodded. 'That's all right. Just buzz when you're ready. There are only a couple waiting, and they're having a good old gossip at the moment, so I doubt they're in a hurry.'

It was such an odd way of working that he couldn't imagine ever getting used to it, although there was something reassuring about the laid-back way this surgery operated, especially after working as a locum in some very high-pressured practices lately.

'Thank you.'

She hovered by the door. 'I'm sorry about yesterday. About being a bit—you know—snippy with you. Can we start again?'

He found he was smiling. 'I'd like that. Thank you. And I'm sorry I was late.'

'You don't have to apologise to me,' she assured him. 'I should let you know that I won't be here on Thursday and Friday. I'm going down to Rochester for a long weekend, but don't worry. Patricia, the head receptionist at Castle Street is covering me.'

He nodded. 'Right, thanks for letting me know. I'm sure we'll manage. Have a lovely time.'

She coloured a little, still hesitating in the doorway. Clearing her throat, she finally said, rather awkwardly, 'Anyway, I'll leave you to it.'

As she headed out of the consulting room, he stared at the coffee on his desk and thought maybe things wouldn't be so bad around here after all.

After a busy morning seeing a stream of cheerful and chatty patients, none of whom had anything really wrong with them, as far as he could tell, but all seeming remarkably eager to learn how he was doing, he left his room and walked into the office.

Beverley was nowhere to be seen, and Anna was sitting at her desk, eating a sandwich. She put it down as soon as he appeared.

'Have you brought anything for lunch? Would you like me to nip out and get you something, or are you going home?'

'I'm popping home to give Mum a hand. She's helping with the unpacking, and no doubt she's already prepared me something to eat. After that I'll get straight out to the visits. Are there many?'

She shook her head. 'Only two. Is Gracie coming home for lunch or is she staying at school?'

He felt his heart thudding. What was her interest in Gracie, suddenly?

'She's staying at school. It's best not to unsettle her by bringing her home halfway through the day.'

He didn't want to go into any more details and hoped she'd change the subject.

She was looking at him with undisguised sympathy, and he felt a prickle of unease.

'It must be so hard for you all. I'm so sorry,' she began.

Indignation flared in him. 'What do you mean by that?'

She looked flustered. 'Well, you know. Just, the way Gracie is.'

'What do you mean, the way Gracie is?'

'I just mean, well, I know how difficult it is for you to get her to school, and I'm sorry I wasn't more sympathetic yesterday. If I'd known I wouldn't have given you such a hard time about being late. Honestly, I do understand—'

'Oh, do you?' He glared at her. 'So, who's been talking? How do you know about the way Gracie was yesterday?'

The roses on her cheeks spread until her entire face looked pink. 'Er, no one. But it's a small village, and she was quite noisy, and—'

'I see.' He shook his head. 'Small villages. Small minds.'

She gasped. 'That's not fair! Just because people notice doesn't mean they're judging you, or Gracie for that matter! Why would they? Why would I? I was just saying that I understood why you were late, and that it must be difficult for you. What's wrong with that?'

There was nothing wrong with it, when he thought about it logically, but he wasn't feeling very logical at that moment. 'Visits.'

'Pardon?'

'Have you got the notes for the visits?'

'Oh. Oh yes.' She rummaged on her desk and handed him two computer printouts. 'Summaries. It's Mrs Clarke and Miss Wilcox. Oh, and can you call at Maudie's for Mrs Clarke? She's low on milk.'

'And I'm the milkman?'

'If you look at her notes you'll see she's having problems with her back again. That's why she can't get out. And—'

'Let me guess. And Daddy wouldn't have minded.'

He grabbed the notes from her hand, doing his best to ignore the look of shock on her face, and left the surgery, closing the door none-too-quietly behind him.

Chapter 5

It was a different world. Rochester was a lovely place, and Anna couldn't fault it. But it wasn't home, and somehow, Lee wasn't—well, Lee.

She'd been to Kent before to visit him, when he was a student at the university, studying for his Master of Sciences in Pharmaceuticals. He'd been living in student accommodation then, and it had been a fun, if slightly weird experience, to mingle with his fellow students and join in with their way of life, which was so far removed from her own.

Now though, Lee was doing a pre-registration year, working in a community pharmacy to enable him to practice as a qualified pharmacist, and he'd moved into a flat in Rochester with a fellow former student, Gary. It seemed much more serious and grown-up, somehow, and brought home to Anna that this wasn't just a temporary situation.

When he'd commenced his degree as a mature student at the tender age of twenty-four, having finally broken it to his parents that he had no desire to take over the family farm, Anna had tried to be reasonable about it. After all, it wouldn't be forever, and it would benefit them both in the long term. She'd always known that Lee wasn't keen on farming as a career, and she was glad for him that he'd finally had the courage to pursue his dream of going to university. Kent was a long way from Yorkshire, but the course would end eventually.

Now, though, it was home for Lee, and before long it would be her home, too. The six-and-a-half-hour journey from Pickering to Rochester had reinforced in her mind how far away from Bramblewick Lee really was, and she realised that, with every mile the train covered, her trepidation had increased.

'You'll love the castle,' Lee had informed her, as he threw his arms around her at the station. 'You love old buildings, and Rochester's full of them. It's practically Dickensville here. Just your sort of thing.'

It would have been, too, if she'd been there on holiday. She had, indeed, loved the beautiful castle, and the cathedral, and the wonderful Dickens exhibits at the Guildhall Museum, but it didn't mean that she wanted to call the town home. It wasn't Bramblewick. She wondered if it would ever feel as dear and as comfortable to her as it clearly did to Lee.

The trip to see him had been arranged months ago, when he and Gary had found the flat. Since moving home and starting work, Lee hadn't been back to Yorkshire once, unlike when he'd been studying. Then he'd come home for every single holiday and had seemed to enjoy being back among his family and friends. This time was clearly different. Anna could see the excitement in his face as he showed her around his adopted home town, and with every passing hour her spirits sank a little lower.

'I know the flat's not up to much,' he'd assured her, opening the door as they'd arrived back from the station, 'but we'll find something better when I can practice, and in the meantime Gary's happy for us to stay here. It will only be for a few months.'

The flat was stark and masculine, but Gary was welcoming and cheerful, and Anna liked him immediately.

He'd cooked for them, and had even laid the table, much to Lee's evident amusement. As they ate spaghetti Bolognese—was that all men could ever cook, Anna wondered—and drank wine, she listened quietly as they chatted and laughed about people she'd never heard of, all the time wondering how she was ever going to integrate herself into this strange new life.

After doing the dishes, at his own insistence, Gary very discreetly left them to it.

'You're not driving me out,' he assured Anna, as she started to protest that he really didn't have to leave on her account. 'I'm meeting some of the lads. It's Thursday night. We always head to The Dog and Duck, don't we Lee?'

Lee nodded. 'Yeah. And most Fridays and Saturdays, too. Tell Josh I haven't forgotten about that tenner. He can buy me a drink next week as interest.'

Gary had laughed and headed out, leaving Lee and Anna sitting in awkward silence. After a few moments, during which she racked her brains, trying to think of something to say, she eventually managed, 'Gary seems nice.'

'Oh, he is. You met him before though. When we were in student accommodation, remember? He lived across the hall.'

She frowned, shaking her head. 'Don't remember. Anyway, it's not a bad flat. Bit small I suppose.'

'You'd be shocked if you knew how much we paid for it. The rent's a lot higher here than it is in Yorkshire. Still, when I'm working properly, I should be able to afford something better.'

'And when I get a job, that'll help.'

Her voice was small. She couldn't imagine finding work down here. It all seemed so alien to her. She thought longingly of the little surgery at Bramblewick. She wondered how Beverley was managing without her. She hoped Connor was okay. How was Gracie doing? She must ask Izzy when she rang her later.

'Yeah, yeah. Sure.'

They were quiet again.

'I found a dress,' Anna told him. 'For the wedding, I mean.'

'Did you? Great.' They both shuffled uncomfortably. 'Would you like a coffee?'

'I don't mind really. Don't go to any trouble on my account.'

'Well, I'm going to have one, so...'

'Oh, in that case, okay. Thanks.'

It was awkward and they looked at each other, stricken.

'It's just because we haven't seen each other for a while,' Lee said suddenly, taking her hand. 'It feels a bit strange doesn't it? But we'll get back to normal before you know it.'

'I'm sure we will,' Anna agreed.

They had a pleasant enough few days together, exploring the delights of Rochester, sometimes with Gary in tow, but mostly alone. Anna soon found out all about Lee's placement and the people he worked with, and which of his fellow ex-students he kept in touch with, and the wild antics at The Dog and Duck, and Gary's on-off relationship with a glamorous physiotherapist called Paula.

'You haven't asked me anything about home,' she remarked as they curled up on the sofa on the Saturday evening. 'Aren't you interested?'

He'd laughed. 'Not much point asking about Bramblewick,' he said. 'Nothing ever changes there, does it?'

She'd felt quite indignant at that remark. 'Actually, things do change all the time. Have you forgotten we have two new members of staff for a start? And you haven't even asked me how I'm getting on living at Izzy's.'

'Well, how are you getting on living at Izzy's?' he said, grinning.

She shrugged. 'All right. We get on really well, actually.'

'Good to hear.'

'Isn't it?' Her eyes flashed. 'And the new receptionist is dismal. And the new doctor is...' Her voice trailed off.

What was the new doctor? Annoying. Unpunctual. Oversensitive. Grumpy. Tired. Worried. Stressed. Caring. Desperately concerned about his daughter.

'The new doctor is what?' Lee sounded amused.

'Very professional,' she said eventually, remembering the telephone conversation she'd had with Izzy on Friday night, as she sat in bed while Lee watched an old episode of *Top Gear* in the living room.

Gracie had apparently had another bad morning at school on the Friday, although she'd completely changed in the afternoon. Ash had taken a music class, and Gracie could evidently sing very well, and clearly loved doing so. She'd apparently been completely entranced by the whole lesson.

'Honestly, she was a different girl, judging by what Ash said,' Izzy assured her. 'Just shows you. Bless her. I suppose it's good that at least music can touch her.' Anna's heart had ached for the little girl, and she'd wondered, if she felt so much for her already, having only just met her, how hard was it for Connor to watch? How did he cope, seeing his daughter locked away somewhere he could rarely reach her? And where in all this was Gracie's mother?

Lee ruffled her hair. 'I do love you, you know.'

She smiled. 'I know you do. Love you too.'

They relaxed against each other and turned their attention back to the television, where some American soldier in World War Two was declaring his passion to a wide-eyed English girl.

As the characters lovingly embraced Anna realised that there'd been very little passion between her and Lee that weekend, which was odd, considering they'd not seen each other for months.

But then, there was more to life than passion, she thought firmly. Lee loved her and she loved him. It had always been that way. Everyone knew they were the perfect couple after all.

Chapter 6

As his mother held out her arms to his daughter, Connor held his breath, wondering what sort of reaction they could expect that morning.

'Happy birthday, Gracie!' she said, ever the optimist.

Reluctantly Gracie allowed herself to be hugged. She made no attempt to hug back, but at least she didn't wriggle or cry out, instead merely looking away, her back rigid. Sometimes, she enjoyed being cuddled. Sometimes, she initiated the cuddles herself. He treasured those moments. They were few and far between.

'Happy birthday, darling.' He risked a cuddle himself, gratified that she seemed more relaxed in his arms.

'I'm nine,' she informed him.

'So you are. All grown up,' he said, smiling.

'I'm not grown up,' she corrected him immediately.

'Well, no, quite right. You're not.' He glanced at his mother who was shaking her head slightly. You had to be very careful what you said to Gracie. Life for her was strictly black or white. There were no grey tones. She didn't understand anything that wasn't absolutely one hundred per cent accurate and honest.

At least she seemed to like her presents, but when her grandmother produced the birthday cake, she shook her head, backing away from it.

'I don't like that,' she announced.

Connor felt for his mother, who had baked it herself while Gracie was at school the previous day.

'Why ever not?' he said gently. 'It's a lovely chocolate cake. You like chocolate cake.'

She shook her head again. 'No. I don't like that.' She pointed at the swirly pink writing on the top of the cake.

'It just says, "Happy birthday, Gracie".' He frowned. 'Why don't you like that?'

She shrugged. 'Don't like it. Can I have my breakfast now?'

'Would you like something different? I've bought you some pancakes and syrup since it's your special day,' his mother said.

Gracie folded her arms. 'Porridge.'

'Porridge. Again. Right.'

Connor touched his mother's arm as she passed him, noting with dismay the glint of tears in her eyes.

'Don't take it to heart, Mum. She doesn't mean anything by it.'

'Oh, I know that, Connor. Of course I know that. It's not me I'm sad for, it's her. Poor little mite.' She bit her lip, then smiled at him far too brightly. 'So, porridge, coming right up.'

As they ate their breakfasts, Connor thought that it wouldn't be much of a birthday for his daughter. She would face the usual drama of being taken to school against her will and spend most of the day there. Then there'd be no cake, and she'd take little interest in her cards and presents, if he knew her. He sighed, then realised that he'd done so and tried to cover it up by asking if there was any tea left in the pot. His mother clearly wasn't fooled.

'We should do something different.' She held up her hand as he started to protest. 'No, I mean it. How about taking her to The Bay Horse for her tea? It's a quiet little pub, from what I've seen of it, and we should get out and about, see people. After all, if this is going to be your new home, you need to start integrating. Besides,' she added firmly, 'it's Gracie's birthday, and we should do something special, no matter what.'

'But the pub? You know what she was like last time.' He tried to suppress a shudder, the memory of Gracie's screams and wails of protest still making him cringe as he remembered the disgusted looks of their fellow diners, and the polite suggestion by the manager that perhaps they would prefer to eat elsewhere, since the restaurant was clearly not to the child's taste.

'You have to start somewhere, Connor,' his mother said, her eyes pleading. 'You can't stay hidden away in this house forever. This is a lovely little village, so why not get yourselves out and about? I'll bet they're dying to meet you both, and you need friends. You need to mix with other people.' She lowered her voice, leaning towards him slightly. 'She can't be your whole life. You need to make friends with people your own age, have a laugh. Have a life.'

He stared into his cup of tea, not really seeing it. He couldn't imagine any kind of life that didn't completely revolve around Gracie's needs. And there really wasn't time for anything—or anyone—else.

'What about the doctor's daughter?'

He blinked, and the amber liquid in the cup swam back into focus. 'What? Anna, you mean? What about her?'

'Why don't you ask her along?'

'Why on earth would I do that?'

'Well, she's the only person you really know in the village after all. And we *are* living in her house. It would be nice, wouldn't it? To get to know her better, I mean. And for her to get to know you and meet Gracie.'

'Mum,' his tone was warning, 'I've told you once. She's leaving soon, and she's getting married in a few weeks.'

'And where is this fiancé of hers? In Kent, isn't he? That's a long way away. I wouldn't count your chickens just yet.'

He almost laughed. She was incorrigible. 'She's actually just spent a few days down there with him. Probably finalised the wedding plans while she was there, and—I don't know—bought new curtains for the marital home or something. You can give up on that idea.'

'What idea?' She raised an eyebrow, obviously trying to look innocent, but he knew her too well. 'All I'm saying is, it would be nice to meet your work colleague at last. Even if she won't be around long. And anyway, she might appreciate the offer. She's been through a tough time, too, you know. It's not all about you.'

As he opened his mouth to protest she winked at him, and he shrugged, defeated. 'All right, I'll ask her. Although I shouldn't imagine for one moment that she'll accept. Things were a little frosty before she went away.'

'Oh? And why's that?'

He swallowed. 'Er, she was asking questions, and I may have overreacted a little.'

'Questions?'

His eyes bored into hers, all too aware of Gracie sitting next to him, spooning porridge into her mouth. His mother nodded. 'Ah, right. Well, even more reason to invite her then. Make amends. Put things on a fresh footing, don't you think?'

'If I must.'

'Yes, my darling boy,' she told him sternly. 'You really must.'

***

'Do I look all right? You don't think this dress is a bit tight?'

Anna surveyed her reflection in the mirror, turning left then right to look at herself from as many different angles as possible. 'I'm sure I've put weight on. That's what a few days in Kent do for your figure. Lee and Gary live off fast food, and they wouldn't let me cook. Apart from one meal of spaghetti Bolognese, I ate nothing but fish and chips, pizza, and burgers.'

Izzy gave her a sly grin. 'Does it matter? About the dress I mean. I thought it was just a quiet birthday tea for Gracie in the local pub?'

Anna spun round. 'It is! What are you getting at?'

'Well, you're very dressed up for tea. And you're wearing lipstick. Ages since I saw you wearing lipstick.'

'I don't know what you're insinuating,' Anna said, flustered. She tugged at her dress, pulled a face, then sank onto the bed. 'Seriously, perhaps I should change. What do you really think?'

'I think you're worrying far too much about what's supposed to be a casual night out at The Bay Horse. I repeat, what does it matter?'

'Well, I'm meeting Connor's mother for the first time for a start,' Anna pointed out.

'And? She's not going to be your mother-in-law is she? What difference does it make?'

'I just don't want her to think... Oh, I don't know. And Connor is my boss after all. I have to keep up appearances.'

'Hmm.' Izzy surveyed her thoughtfully. 'How did you and Lee get on, Anna?'

Anna frowned. 'What do you mean by that? Very well, as we always do. Why wouldn't we?'

'He must have been thrilled to see you. I expect you had an awful lot of catching up to do.'

'Well, yes. He had loads to tell me. He's really enjoying life down there. He loves the work he's doing, and he's made so many friends.'

'But that's not what I meant. I meant, catching up. You know.' Her voice was heavy with meaning, and Anna blushed.

'Yeah, of course. That, too.'

Although, they'd done such a lot of sightseeing, and Lee had wanted to introduce her to some of his friends, and then Gary had been around a lot. Besides, there was plenty of time for all that after they were married.

Wasn't there?

She realised suddenly that there were only a few weeks to the big day, and she still hadn't finalised the cake.

'I need to call at the café tomorrow,' she said flatly. 'I have a cake to organise.'

Izzy watched her, her eyes expressing something that Anna didn't really want to acknowledge.

'You still haven't done that? Honestly, this is the most casual wedding I've ever heard of. You have got the reception sorted?'

'Of course. The back room in the Bay Horse. A buffet for twenty people. Ernie and Sandra have got it all written down. I have my dress. I'll sort the cake tomorrow. That's everything, isn't it?'

'Flowers? Cars? Photographer? Rings?'

'I'm using Mum's ring, remember?'

Izzy's eyes softened. 'Of course. Sorry. What about Lee?'

'He doesn't want a ring. I offered to have Dad's altered, but he said not to bother. And I'm not wasting money on flowers, it's only a registry office wedding, after all. As for cars, I'll book a taxi.'

'A taxi? Oh, the glamour!'

'It will do the job,' Anna laughed. 'And there are plenty of people who can take photographs. After all, nearly everyone has a camera on their phone these days.'

'But this isn't what you wanted is it?' Izzy said gently. 'You used to dream about your wedding when we were teenagers. This certainly wasn't the sort of thing you had in mind.'

'It's different now,' Anna pointed out. 'It wouldn't be the same without Dad.'

'Are you sure, Anna?' Izzy asked. 'I mean, that it's just losing your dad that's making you downgrade this wedding so drastically? There's nothing else?'

Anna bristled. 'Of course not. What on earth would make you say that?'

'Just that, well, there doesn't seem to be much enthusiasm, on your part at least. What about Lee? Did he seem excited about the wedding?'

Anna felt her face burning. 'Of course. We talked about it a lot.'

'Okay. Sorry. Just checking. Well anyway, you look lovely. Go and have a great time with that hunky doctor.'

'And his mother and daughter.'

'Yeah, shame about that.'

Anna tutted and waved her engagement ring in Izzy's face. 'Sometimes I think you're determined to lead me astray.'

Izzy held her gaze, unblinking. It was Anna who turned away first.

Chapter 7

Ernie was all smiles as Anna entered The Bay Horse. 'All right, love? I wasn't expecting you tonight. What can I get you?'

Anna was about to explain that she was meeting the Blake family, and enquire if they had arrived, but a sudden commotion behind her answered that question. As she glanced round she saw other heads turn to survey the little family in the corner.

A middle-aged woman in a navy-blue coat was trying to persuade Gracie to sit down, and Connor was obviously trying to tell her not to waste her time, while making vain attempts to calm Gracie. Anna's heart went out to them all, yet at the same time she felt suddenly awkward. How could she go over there while they were dealing with that?

Ernie leaned over the bar and murmured, 'You're meeting Dr Blake? Took him five minutes to get that kid in here, she was creating such a fuss. Spoilt little madam, isn't she? I know what I'd do if she was mine.'

Anna wanted to explain, to make Ernie understand,

but it was none of her business, and not her place to tell anyone about Gracie's condition. As she was wondering what to do, Connor glanced up and his eyes met hers. She saw the look of desperation in them and melted. Taking a deep breath she strode over to the table.

'Hello.' If she'd hoped, somewhere in the back of her mind, that her voice would calm Gracie, she was mistaken. The child continued wriggling and crying, protesting loudly about something that Anna couldn't make out.

Connor jumped up. 'Give me five minutes,' he said to no one in particular, and dashed out of the pub.

Anna felt bewildered, and her feelings obviously communicated themselves to Mrs Blake.

'I'm so sorry, dear. I take it you're Anna? I'm Dottie.'

Anna wasn't surprised, given the stress she was under. Then she realised that Dottie was the woman's name.

'How do you do. Er, should we leave? Has Connor gone? What's happening?'

Gracie, amazingly, suddenly stopped squealing and stared at her. Anna smiled gently, hoping that the unexpected peace would last, but within a few seconds Gracie was dragging at her grandmother's hand again and begging to leave.

'I'm so sorry about this,' Mrs Blake said, her face

pink, whether with exhaustion or embarrassment, Anna wasn't sure. 'It's the material, you see. She really can't cope with it, and we forgot her cover. So stupid of us. Connor won't be long.'

Anna dropped into a chair and frowned.

'Material?'

'The chairs,' Mrs Blake explained. 'They're all wrong, and—oh, here's Connor now, thank goodness.'

Connor rushed in, carrying what looked like a duvet cover in his hands. Carefully he draped it over the entire chair before calmly pointing it out to his daughter, patting the seat and coaxing her to sit down.

To Anna's relief and surprise, Gracie cautiously sank onto the chair and there was a moment's hushed silence as it seemed every single person in the pub held their breath. Gracie wiped her face, which was thankfully turning from a shade of deep red back to its normal colour, and then sniffed, but didn't make any other sound.

Anna realised she'd also been holding her breath and slowly exhaled.

Connor sat down, rubbed his forehead then picked up a menu and hid his face behind it.

Anna wondered what on earth was going on, and glanced across at Mrs Blake, who gave her a pleading look and patted her hand. As she noticed the menu shaking beside her, Anna realised that Connor was trembling, and it occurred to her that he was hiding behind the menu, rather than reading it. She had to stop herself from reaching out to give his arm a reassuring squeeze. He must be mortified, and how distressing for him to see his daughter in such a state.

She looked across at Gracie who was looking fixedly at the salt pot on the table, her expression revealing nothing about her current state of mind. Anna wasn't sure how long peace would hold. Perhaps it might be a good thing to get the meal over and done with as soon as possible. Reaching over she picked up another menu.

'Can you recommend anything, Anna?' Mrs Blake's voice was choked, and Anna could see she was on the verge of tears. This wasn't at all the sort of evening she'd imagined. Was this what it was always like?

'The scampi's usually good,' she said, casting a sideways glance at Connor's hands. 'Or there's the lamb with redcurrant jelly. That's very tasty.'

Connor put down the menu and cleared his throat.

'The lamb sounds perfect. Mum?'

'Goodness, give me a minute. I haven't really looked at all the options yet.'

'What about you, Gracie?' He turned to his daughter and gave her an encouraging smile. 'What about fishfingers?'

'I don't like fishfingers,' Gracie announced.

Mrs Blake sighed. 'You do like fishfingers, darling. You had them all the time when you were staying at my house, remember?' She murmured to Anna, 'It was all she would eat to be honest.'

Gracie slowly started to shake her head. 'I don't like fishfingers.'

'All right, all right. You don't like fishfingers.' Connor nodded. 'Okay, so what would you like?'

'Why did she say I like them when I don't?' Gracie demanded.

'Grandma didn't mean anything by it,' Connor assured her. 'She just got mixed up.'

'But Grandma's always saying I like things when I don't. She made me a cake with horrible pink writing on it and she said I would like it, but I don't like it. I told her I don't like it and she didn't believe me.'

'I just didn't see what there was to dislike,' Mrs Blake said, sounding desperate. 'I didn't say I didn't believe you.'

'But I told you I didn't like it, and you said I did, so that means you think I'm lying. And I just told you I don't like fishfingers and you said I did, so that means you think I'm lying about that as well.'

'No, no. I'm not saying that—'

'Leave it, Mum,' Connor said, keeping his voice even.

'But I'm not calling her a liar. I'm just saying she

liked fishfingers when she stayed at my house, that's all.'

'I didn't.'

'And you liked pancakes, too, but this morning you wouldn't even try them. So you see, it's not that you lie, just that your tastes change.'

'You're always trying to make me eat things I don't like,' Gracie wailed.

Anna looked around as she heard someone at the next table say, quite loudly, 'That child wants discipline. I've never heard anything like it.'

She didn't recognise the couple who were sitting smugly with their own well-behaved children, but she could have cheerfully throttled them.

Connor's head turned and his mouth opened. Anna had an awful feeling he was about to say something, but if he was, he was stopped in his tracks as a loud crash came from the kitchen.

'Oops, that's the chef sacked,' called someone cheerfully.

Gracie covered her ears with her hands and began to rock backwards and forwards.

'What on earth is she doing now?' said the man at the next table.

Their two not-so-well-behaved children began to giggle and mimic Gracie, as Anna's face heated with anger. Who did they think they were, making fun of the poor girl?

Connor stood up. 'We're going. Come on.'
'Connor!'

He took no notice of his mother's pleas but reached for Gracie's hand and pulled her gently to her feet.

'Come on, sweetheart. We're going home.'

He grabbed the duvet cover from the chair and threw it over his shoulder.

'I'm sorry about this,' he said to Anna, then strode out of the pub, taking his daughter with him.

Mrs Blake shook her head. 'I'm so sorry, dear. Looks like it's dinner at ours. Would you join us?'

'Oh, really, it's okay. I'll just go home.' Anna felt the last thing Connor needed was for her to turn up at the house, compounding his humiliation.

'Please.' She sounded desperate. 'If you go home it will be twice as bad for him tomorrow at work. Can you just come back with us, let us turn this evening around? Let him see that you're okay with this, that it hasn't turned you against them.'

'Turned me against them?' Anna was baffled. 'Why would it turn me against them?'

Mrs Blake held her gaze for a moment. 'Some people can't cope, and some people shun them rather than deal with it all. I know it's difficult, believe me, but Gracie is a good girl. Underneath it all, she's a good girl. Please believe that.'

'I do, honestly. Don't get upset,' Anna said, horrified

to see tears in the woman's eyes. 'Look, I'll come back if you're sure Connor won't mind.'

'He won't. I mean, he might seem a bit embarrassed at first, but believe me, it's what he needs more than anything. Thank you, Anna.'

***

Tea turned out to be shepherd's pie, carrots, and broccoli, all taken from the freezer and hastily shoved in the oven, or a pan of boiling water, by Mrs Blake, while Connor settled Gracie who, sitting on the sofa staring wide-eyed at the screen as the cast of *Phantom of the Opera* performed a miracle, seemed much happier.

'It was the dralon that started it,' Mrs Blake explained, as they tucked in to their meal at the table, while Gracie ate hers off a tray on her lap.

'I'm sorry?'

'I'm sure Anna doesn't need to know all the details,' Connor said, prodding at a carrot despondently. 'Suffice it to say that now she knows what it can be like. I'm sure that's enough.'

'Don't be silly, Connor,' said Mrs Blake. 'What it is, dear,' she continued, 'is the material. She can't bear the feel of it against her skin. Very sensitive to different materials, she is, so we usually bring the cotton duvet cover out with us for her to sit on, but we clean forgot, and that kicked it all off.'

'I see.'

'If it hadn't been that it would have been the loud conversation, or the smells from the food, or the people she didn't like the look of.' Connor sounded weary.

'That family at the next table were disgraceful,' Mrs Blake said.

'You're right, they were.' Anna had wanted to rage at them herself, so she could imagine how hard it had been for Connor to keep his temper.

'I told you. What can you expect from a village this size?' Connor said, stabbing at some broccoli quite viciously.

'Excuse me,' Anna said indignantly, 'but I didn't even recognise that family. They're certainly not locals. Don't judge Bramblewick by people like them.'

'But that's what I said would happen,' he said earnestly. 'In a small village, everyone knows your business. How is someone like Gracie ever going to fit in?'

'For goodness' sake.' Anna put down her fork. 'She's not some sort of monster that has to be hidden away!'

'I never said she was,' he said, clearly angry.

'She's just a child. A little girl with some problems. No one's going to think badly of her. Anyone would think you're expecting all the villagers to turn up with pitchforks and torches.'

Mrs Blake beamed at her. 'Exactly. I've been telling him all along that he needs to stop hiding away. He must get out there and meet people. Let them get to know the pair of them.'

'Yes, he must. Let the villagers get used to you, and to Gracie. They'll be welcoming. Why don't you give them a chance?'

He pushed his plate away. 'In my experience, all they do is judge.'

'You mean like you are now?'

'I'm sorry?'

'Well, isn't that what you're doing? Judging them? You've convinced yourself that they're going to react in a certain way, and you're not going to give them the chance to prove otherwise. Don't you think that's a bit unfair? Not to mention hypocritical.'

'Well!'

Mrs Blake laughed. 'I knew I was going to like you,' she said. 'She's quite right,' she told her son. 'You can sit there with a face like a wet weekend for as long as you like, but she's got you sussed. Let's be honest.'

Connor gaped at them both for a moment, then to Anna's relief his face relaxed into a grin.

'Okay. Point taken.'

She stared at him in amazement. He looked so different when he smiled, and so much younger. He had quite a cheeky grin. His brown eyes twinkled, and she realised she was smiling back at him. She felt a funny little flutter in her stomach and didn't quite know how to deal with the sudden rush of emotion she was experiencing.

As she stepped out into the street later that evening, she turned her face up to the night sky, glad of the cool air that took the heat from her skin. She seemed to have been burning up for the last hour or so, as she and Connor sat beside Gracie on the sofa and watched *Beauty and the Beast* with her.

Gracie knew every word and spoke Belle's lines along with her. Each time a character broke into song, Gracie followed suit, and she had a lovely clear voice, and seemingly no inhibitions about singing in front of Anna. She'd even got up at one point, twirling round the room as Belle and the Beast waltzed, and Anna watched her in fascination.

'She's really good,' she whispered to Connor. 'And she certainly enjoys it, doesn't she?'

'She adores music and dancing,' he whispered back. 'She's at her happiest when she's watching something like this. It's as if it reaches through to her when nothing and no one else can.'

'She's a lovely little girl,' she'd replied. 'It's wonderful to see her so happy and relaxed.'

He'd smiled at her again, and she'd had that funny

sensation in her stomach once more. As he sat beside her on the sofa, she felt every nerve end was jangling. He was so close to her, and it was having an unexpected effect on her. As soon as the film ended she stood up and made her farewells.

Mrs Blake had enfolded her in a hug, and even Gracie had smiled at her and said goodbye, which Anna felt was a real breakthrough, although she suspected it was more down to the magic of Disney than anything she'd done or said. Connor had shown her out, suddenly awkward again as he opened the door for her.

'Well, er, thank you for being so understanding. Sorry about dinner.'

'There was nothing wrong with dinner,' she assured him. 'I love shepherd's pie.'

He gave her a sheepish smile. 'You know what I mean. But thanks. Really.'

Gulping, she'd managed a faint, 'That's all right. I'll see you tomorrow,' before rushing out through the door.

Arriving back at Rose Cottage, she was greeted by an eager Izzy.

'Ooh, how did it go?'

'Well...'

Half an hour later, Izzy was up to speed with the events of the evening, and she and Anna sat drinking wine and musing on the whole Gracie situation.

'I told you she was musical,' Izzy said. 'She really seems to open up when she sings.'

'And dances,' Anna added. 'She's quite a little mover, bless her. It's all quite amazing really when you think of how she behaved in the pub. The difference was startling. I felt so bad for Connor. He was mortified, and he seemed so desperate to make her happy and give her a nice birthday treat.'

'So,' Izzy said, with a wry smile, 'things aren't so frosty between you anymore?'

'It seems not,' Anna confirmed. 'He's actually really nice when you get to know him.'

'And I was right about the other thing, wasn't I?'

'What other thing?'

'Doctor Dreamboat. He's rather gorgeous, isn't he?'

'I suppose so.' There was no way on earth that Anna was going to admit the reaction she'd had to Connor that evening.

'Still,' said Izzy, yawning, 'that doesn't affect you, does it? I mean, you've got Lee. Why would you even notice Connor?'

'Exactly.'

And there was no way that Anna was going to admit the other matter to her friend. It was hard enough to admit it to herself. But there was no denying that it had been a long time since she'd felt that fluttering in her stomach, that frisson of excitement, that physical longing for someone. In fact, she couldn't remember when it had happened before, and, given that she'd just spent a few days with her fiancé, that really was a matter for concern.

Chapter 8

It had been a busy week at the surgery, and Anna was quite glad to have reached Friday. She was also relieved to have made it almost to the weekend without having a row with Beverley, who clearly wasn't taking the job seriously. She was frequently late and seemed bored by the whole thing.

Although she often looked as if she was busy, when Anna checked what she was doing, she seemed to be spending a lot of time staring at the appointments screen, clicking the computer mouse as if to look like she was actually doing something, or shuffling papers on her desk.

Anna seemed to be constantly explaining the same things over and over to her, and it was obvious that Beverley was taking nothing in. How could she possibly have worked in a surgery before?

It was Trev, the chemist's delivery driver, who shed light on the matter. Many patients were signed up with chemists, who would send drivers out to the surgeries in the area to collect prescriptions and bring them back to the pharmacies, then deliver the medication to the patients.

Trev was one of Bramblewick's regular drivers, coming in nearly every day, but he'd been on holiday and had only got back on the Wednesday afternoon. She hadn't seen him on the Thursday, his first day back at work, as she'd been in the back office, leaving Beverley to deal with reception on her own, but on Friday she'd left Beverley supposedly scanning and was at the front desk when he walked in.

Flashing him a cheery smile, she remarked on his golden tan.

'Looks like you had a great time in Spain.'

'Smashing,' he acknowledged. 'It was a bit dodgy at first, mind, but when we chummed up with Ned and Vera from Wolverhampton they showed us this great little café that did a first-class egg and chips. After that, we were fine.'

Anna laughed. 'Not one for traditional Spanish food then?'

Trev pulled a face. 'Didn't fancy trying it. You never know what they put in there do you? I mean, squid! Ugh!' He shook his head. 'Give me egg and chips and a warm beer any day. Hey, I see you've been landed with Dolly Daydream.'

Anna frowned. 'Who?'

'Beverley.' He leaned over the counter, lowering his

voice. 'She used to work at The Willows surgery in Helmston. What's she doing here?'

'She's my replacement,' Anna said, trying to suppress a sigh. 'Although I'm not sure she's going to be ready in time. I'm worried sick.'

'Not surprised.' He shook his head. 'She was rubbish.'

'She was?' Anna raised an eyebrow. 'How do you know?'

'Because the lasses at The Willows used to moan about her constantly. She wasn't interested in the work. Downright lazy she was. They were glad to see the back of her. Can't believe you've taken her on. How did she convince you?'

'She didn't,' Anna said. 'I didn't even get to meet her. It was the practice manager at Castle Street who interviewed her.'

Trev pursed his lips. 'Reckon The Willows gave her a glowing reference just to get rid of her. Can't believe you're landed with her. She'll never be able to cope here on her own after you've gone.' He winked. 'Maybe it's a sign.'

'A sign? Of what?'

'That you're not supposed to leave Bramblewick.' He grinned as she gave him a knowing look. 'All right, but you can't blame me for trying. It won't be the same here without you. There should always be a Gray here.

I'll miss you, and I won't be the only one.'

'Oh, Trev, don't.' Anna blinked her eyes, quickly dismissing the tears that had sprung up. 'Bramblewick will be fine without me. Beverley or no Beverley.'

As she glanced at the clock though, noting that Beverley was once again late back from lunch, she wasn't so sure that Bramblewick would cope after all. Maybe she should speak to the manager. Tell him of her concerns. No doubt he would have checked if she'd been working at the Castle Street branch, but he showed little interest in what was going on out here. She only ever really found out what was happening when one of the nurses turned up to run a clinic and filled her in with the latest gossip.

She straightened as she heard the outer door open and footsteps in the corridor. As Connor entered the office she started in surprise.

'I wasn't expecting you back so soon. How did it go?'

He'd been called in for a 'friendly' meeting with the practice manager to discuss how things were going, and how he was settling in. They'd both expected it to be a simple box-ticking exercise, so Anna was surprised to see the concern evident in his expression.

'Not good. Not good at all.'

'What?' She watched, shocked, as he sank into the chair at the opposite desk to hers and rubbed his forehead. 'What's happened?'

'I really can't believe it,' he admitted, shaking his head. 'It was all very pleasant at first. As you said, a box-ticking exercise more than anything. How was I settling? How did I find the work? Then the tone changed, almost imperceptibly at first. It dawned on me that the meeting wasn't so much about me, but about this place.'

Anna paled. 'What do you mean?'

'I mean, he seemed to be questioning me more on what I thought of this surgery, the way it's run, the problems a small, out-of-the-way surgery like this generates. And then he sprang it on me.'

Anna hardly dare ask. 'Sprang what on you?'

Connor took a deep breath. 'They're considering closing the branch surgery down, Anna. This place, they think it's a waste of time and effort. They asked me if I'd have any objections to working at the main surgery.'

'But—but they can't do that!' Anna leapt to her feet. 'This is the lifeblood of the community. People round here can't be trailing all the way to Helmston to see a doctor! When is this supposed to be happening?'

'He said it was just an idea they were mulling over. He said the other GPs felt that it was a drain on resources, and that selling this building would bring in much-needed income.'

'But don't you have a say in this?' she demanded.

'Surely your opinion counts for something?' Her eyes narrowed suspiciously. 'You didn't agree with them?'

'I'm not a partner yet,' he pointed out. 'Six months as a salaried GP, we agreed, then a partnership if I felt the place suited me.'

'You didn't answer my question,' she said. 'You didn't agree with them did you?'

'Not entirely, no,' he said.

She heard the note of caution in his voice and glared at him. 'What did you say?'

'Look, I agree that it's a long way for patients to travel to Helmston, and I said as much. I did, however, agree that this place needs a shake-up. Well it does,' he protested as she let out an exclamation of disgust. 'However much you might want to preserve it as a shrine to your father, it needs to move on.'

'How dare you?' Anna could barely believe her ears. 'A shrine to my father? He doesn't need a shrine! He'll always be remembered by all the patients here who relied on him, and on this place, and were never let down. You've just betrayed them all. Not just my father, but each and every person who comes to this surgery. I hope you're satisfied.'

'Calm down, Anna,' he said. 'You're blowing this all out of proportion. I never said I wanted it to close. I merely expressed an opinion.'

'That this surgery is an outdated museum piece.

Thanks very much.'

His expression hardened. 'Clearly you're not going to listen to me.'

'You've already said far more than I wanted to hear,' she snapped.

He stood up. 'I'm going for some lunch before afternoon surgery. I'll speak to you later when you're not so hysterical.'

'Don't you dare patronise me! Just because I care, and you don't!'

He stopped at the door; his fingers curled over the handle.

'If this place closes and I have to move to Castle Street it will be a disaster for Gracie. Either I'll have to get someone else to take her to school, or I'll have to move to Helmston, or maybe back home to be closer to my mother, which means uprooting her yet again and making her start at another school, settle into another house. Either way, it's going to be a nightmare, but you didn't think about that, did you? You know, I don't see how you've got the right to hurl abuse at me. This place obviously doesn't matter that much to you. After all, you're the one who's walking out on it. You won't even be around to see what happens to it, so I think it's a bit rich that you're being so aggressive towards me.'

He left the room and Anna sank back in her chair,

stunned at his cheek. Of course she cared, and of course she had the right to be angry and concerned. Didn't she?

But as his words sank in she felt a sudden coldness inside. It would be awful for Connor and Gracie if things changed yet again. And he was right. She was the one leaving after all. Now she felt as if she was abandoning Bramblewick Surgery to its fate. How could she possibly live with that?

***

'There's another one at the desk,' Beverley announced, her tone displaying her disgust. 'Honestly, talk about an overreaction. So, they might have to go to Helmston to see a doctor. Big deal. This is my job we're talking about, but they obviously don't care about that.'

Anna glared at her. Selfish little madam. A lot of these patients were elderly, and the hourly bus service to Helmston would be too much for some of them, especially in the winter.

Doctors at the main surgery did things by the book. There would be no home visits unless the patient was physically unable to get to Helmston. It wouldn't matter that elderly or ill people would be standing at a bus stop, waiting for a bus to arrive, then endure over an hour's journey to town, plus a walk to the surgery on

Castle Street. There'd certainly be no grocery delivery service for them anymore, that was for sure.

But more than that, even, there'd be no meeting place for them to sit and chat. No reassurance that there was somewhere to come if they had any worries or concerns at all. No guarantee that a place would be found for them, and a friendly and concerned ear would always listen to them, no matter how trivial the problem might be.

Connor, she'd quickly discovered, may not appreciate acting as a delivery boy, but he was a good, caring, doctor, and had patience in spades. He reminded her of her father in that respect.

'Dratted survey,' she muttered as she hurried through to the reception to console and reassure yet another worried patient. The practice manager, in his infinite wisdom, had sent out a letter to all the Bramblewick patients, explaining the possible closure of the branch, and enclosing a survey, asking them all to fill it in so they could gauge reactions and come up with solutions to any problems patients might encounter, should the closure go ahead.

Inevitably that had set up a wave of panic in the village, and Anna had been inundated with frightened and angry people waving the pieces of paper at her, and begging her to tell them it was all some horrible mistake.

She really wished she could tell them that, but as she faced an irate Mr Peterson over the counter, she realised that every word she was saying was based on hope, rather than hard facts. Maybe, she thought, Connor would be better off speaking to them. After all, he'd had the actual conversation with the manager. He might be able to offer some constructive advice. If nothing else, he would speak with a clear head, whereas she was a muddle of guilt, confusion, and depression—not least because of the way their once-blossoming friendship seemed right back at square one, thanks to her unwarranted attack on him.

After finally managing to reassure Mr Peterson that she would do everything in her power to persuade the boss to change his mind, and convincing him to fill in the survey giving his full and honest opinion without resorting to profanities, she hurried back into the office and reached for her now lukewarm coffee.

'Is Connor in his consulting room?' she asked, noticing it was gone nine.

'He's not coming.' Beverley spooned some yoghurt into her mouth and then scowled as the phone rang. 'You'll have to wait, mate. I'm eating my breakfast.'

'For goodness sake!' Anna transferred the call to her desk and made the booking for an appointment. Replacing the receiver, she frowned at Beverley. 'What do you mean he's not coming? Since when?'

'Oh, I forgot to tell you. He rang in sick. He's got flu.'

'You're joking!'

Beverley looked blank. 'Why would I joke? Thought it was man flu but, to be fair, he did sound really rough.'

She clearly saw the look of horror on Anna's face, and held up her hands, saying smugly, 'No need to look like that. He'd already rung Castle Street. They're sending a locum. Should be here any minute.'

'But what about Gracie?' The truth was the surgery hadn't been the first thing she'd thought of. Dottie had returned home a few days ago, earlier than planned, as her own mother had been taken ill and she was rushing off to care for her. If Connor really had the flu—and being a doctor, he should surely know—then who was taking Gracie to school? Who was taking care of them both?

She found out after surgery. Having called Izzy, during what she'd known would be playtime at the primary school, she'd learned that Gracie hadn't turned up, and Dr Blake had called to tell them he wasn't well enough to bring her in.

Explaining the situation to her, Anna informed her friend that she'd be late home, as she was going to visit and see how things were.

How things were turned out to be worse than she'd expected.

Gracie opened the door, which was surprising, and she was clearly distressed.

'Daddy's poorly,' she told Anna, her voice tremulous. 'I can't go to school.'

'May I come in?' Anna asked. 'I might be able to help.'

To her great relief, Gracie didn't even hesitate. She nodded and ran back into the living room, leaving Anna to close the door, rather nervously, behind her.

Half expecting to find Connor heading out to tell her they didn't need her help, she was completely taken aback to find him lying on the sofa, wrapped in a blanket. His hair was soaked in sweat, his face was pasty, and he looked terrible.

'You're really ill!'

As if she hadn't truly believed it, which, she supposed, she hadn't. He was too strong, too assured, to be ill after all. Except that he clearly was ill, and in need of help. Well, that was why she was there, wasn't it?

He half opened his eyes, but even that seemed like too much effort for him. He closed them again, murmuring, 'Gracie. Hungry.'

'Have you eaten today, Gracie?' Anna crouched down as the little girl sat on the floor beside her father, staring at him with worried eyes.

Gracie nodded. 'I made some porridge. I know how

to do it. I watched Grandma and Daddy do it. It's easy in the microwave. I've had porridge three times today. I'm quite hungry again now though. I don't think I want porridge again.'

'I'll make you something else,' Anna assured her. 'What about Daddy? Has he eaten anything?'

Gracie's eyes fixed on the wall behind Anna. 'I tried to make him eat porridge but he didn't want it. He wasn't hungry.'

'Has he drunk anything?'

Gracie considered. 'He had some water this morning. He had to telephone people about work and he was drinking water. He couldn't lift the kettle so he couldn't have tea.'

Anna managed a smile. 'Well, never mind. I'm here now. I'll make him something to eat and drink, and I think we should try to get him to bed, don't you?' She stood and headed into the kitchen, surprised to find Gracie following her.

'He should be in bed,' Gracie agreed. 'But I can't stay down here by myself. I'm not old enough.'

'Well, no, but you won't be by yourself, because I'll be here, and I'll stay here.' Anna looked into the fridge, wondering what the little girl would eat, and what, if anything, Connor could manage.

'You can't stay here,' Gracie said. 'You don't live here anymore, and you have to work.'

She had a point, but seeing the state Connor was in, and knowing how demanding Gracie was at the best of times, Anna didn't see she had an option.

'Look, how would you feel if I brought some things over and slept in the spare room? Then I could take you to school and make sure your daddy was okay. Would that be all right with you?'

'I expect so,' Gracie confirmed. 'I can't look after him. I can't lift him up and I can't cook, so I think I will need someone to help me. You can do that.'

'Thank you,' Anna said, relieved. 'So, what do you want to eat?'

She rolled her eyes as Gracie replied, without hesitation, 'Fishfingers.'

Chapter 9

In the end, Anna spent a whole week at Chestnut House. It felt good to be back home—as she considered the house to be, and probably always would—but it was exhausting, taking care of Connor and Gracie.

Luckily, Izzy had stepped in to help. When Anna popped home that first night to grab some things, she'd immediately offered to take Gracie to school every morning and bring her home again afterwards.

It hadn't been easy, as Gracie had taken exception to the idea of going to school at all, and leaving her father behind, but she'd soon settled once she'd settled into the classroom and started work, and she'd become a lot calmer as the days passed and she realised her father was being cared for, tea would be on the table, and there'd be someone sitting with her every evening who would allow her to watch her favourite films and then take her up to bed.

It helped that Anna happily agreed that the bedside lamp should be left on all night, and willingly checked every cupboard and drawer in the bedroom, before closing each door firmly behind her. These little rituals seemed to appease Gracie, so it was well worth the extra time and effort.

Connor had barely eaten or drunk a thing for the first couple of days, and had seemed worried sick, but he'd calmed down a lot when he realised Anna was taking care of the house and his daughter, and by the fourth day he was looking a bit better and was managing some soup and plenty of fluids.

Anna sat on the edge of the bed on Saturday morning, handing him a mug of tea.

'I've brought you some toast up today. See if you can manage that,' she said cheerfully.

'Where's Gracie?' His first question of the day was always about her, Anna realised. He was a very caring father, just as her own had been. She could almost sense Dr Gray's presence in this room, which had once been her parents' bedroom. She reached over and brushed a strand of hair away from Connor's eyes.

'Downstairs watching *Matilda*. She's got a tray on her lap. You won't believe this but she's eating toast.'

Connor stared at her. 'Instead of porridge?'

She nodded, grinning. 'I was making you some, and she asked if she could have the same as you. I was pretty stunned, to be honest, but hey, she's eating it.'

He shook his head slightly, then took another sip of

tea.

He was quiet for a moment, then said in a rather shaky voice, 'Thank you, Anna. I don't know what we'd have done without you.'

'It's no trouble. It's been nice being back here, and Gracie's been no bother.'

'Really?' He looked at her, clearly concerned. 'Are you just saying that?'

'No, honestly.' She shrugged. 'She was a bit awkward about going to school at first, but that's to be expected. She didn't want to leave you for a start. But Izzy's been taking her every morning, and she says it's taking much less time every day to settle her at school. She's working really well in the classroom, too. Her teacher's full of praise for her.'

'That's wonderful.' He was clearly exhausted, and she took the cup from his hands and placed it on the bedside table. He leaned back into his pillow, his face still pale. 'It seems unfair. You have enough to do. The wedding—it's not long now, is it? You must have things…'

His voice trailed off, and she thought it probably a good thing that he was too tired to pursue the subject. She didn't know what she could say, given the rather uncomfortable conversation she'd had on the telephone with Lee last night. Discovering that he was on the way out with his friends again had infuriated her.

It hadn't been a pleasant call.

'Do you think you can manage any toast?' she said softly, feeling a rush of concern for Connor.

'Maybe later. Just leave it there. Thank you.' He frowned suddenly. 'What day is it today?'

'Saturday.'

'Saturday?' He struggled to sit up. 'You'll have Gracie at home all day. I should get up. You'll need help.'

'I won't need help, and you most certainly will not get up,' she said firmly. 'I'm going to take her out for a walk around the village. Maybe we'll go to the Twidales' farm.'

It had been a while since she'd seen Lee's parents, and guilt was eating away at her. Taking Gracie would hopefully provide a good excuse to see them again, without having to go into much detail about Lee.

'She might like to see the animals. Anyway, some fresh air will do her good.'

'She might not like...' His voice trailed off, and without even thinking about it she squeezed his hand.

'Please don't worry. I'll take care of her. She'll be fine.'

His eyes met hers, and she felt that now familiar fluttering in her stomach again.

'I don't know what to say.'

'You don't have to say anything. All you have to do

is get better, and try to eat some of that toast while we're gone, okay? If not, well, not to worry. I can soon rustle up something else for lunch.'

He gave her a faint smile and closed his eyes. She stood up and watched him for a moment, until the change in his breathing reassured her that he'd fallen asleep.

Bending slightly, she kissed him gently on the forehead then rushed out of the bedroom, shocked at her own audacity, and wondering what on earth was happening to her.

***

The trip to Twidale's Farm, on the outskirts of the village, didn't go as well as Anna had hoped.

All had seemed fine as they crossed the bridge over the beck and made their way along the footpath through the fields. The sheep grazing close by hadn't fazed Gracie at all, so she had no cause to suspect how the little girl would react when reaching the farm.

Lee's father, Julian, was more than happy to see her.

'We don't see enough of you,' he said, putting an arm around Anna's shoulders.

'Well, that's because you're both so healthy,' Anna said, laughing. It was true that they enjoyed good health and seldom entered the surgery, but Anna knew she should have visited the farm more often. After all, it was only a ten or fifteen-minute walk from home.

Lee's mother, Jane, appeared at the farmhouse door.

'Anna, how lovely to see you! And who's this young lady?' she enquired, smiling broadly at Gracie.

Gracie refused to look at either of them, studying the barn door instead.

Jane and Julian raised eyebrows and glanced at Anna, who shook her head slightly.

'This is Gracie,' she said, almost apologetically.

'Pleased to meet you, Gracie,' said Jane cheerily. 'Are you both coming inside for a cup of tea?'

'That would be lovely,' Anna said. 'Would you like a drink, Gracie?'

Gracie said nothing, continuing to stare fixedly at the barn door. Anna tried again. 'Jane makes a lovely cup of tea.'

'Or I have some blackcurrant cordial,' Jane offered. 'No one can resist that. Would you like to try a glass?'

Gracie didn't reply and Anna nudged her gently. 'Gracie?'

'I'm not going in there,' said Gracie flatly, still not looking at anyone.

Jane looked quite startled. 'I have biscuits,' she said coaxingly.

Gracie folded her arms. 'I want to go home.'

'Well now,' Julian said, sounding extra hearty,

'you've only just got here. Wouldn't you like to see some of the animals?'

'No thank you.'

'Really? Not even the hens?'

'No thank you.'

'The cows?'

'No.'

'Oh, right.' Julian looked a bit flummoxed. 'Well, I'd better get on with my work. I'll see you again soon I hope, Anna?'

'You will, Julian. Promise.'

Anna felt awkward. She hadn't expected Gracie to revert to this manner when she'd been behaving so much better all week. She supposed she should have been prepared, though. It wasn't Gracie's fault after all.

Suddenly a black and white dog shot over to them and Gracie squealed.

'It's all right, love,' Jane soothed. 'It's just Jacko, our old sheepdog.'

Anna held her breath as Gracie tentatively reached out a hand and stroked the dog, who immediately rolled over to have his tummy tickled. Gracie giggled and began to tickle him. Anna felt quite weak with relief.

'Loves kiddies, he does,' Jane told her. 'Seems like the feeling's mutual.' She nodded meaningfully at Gracie, who was smiling broadly as she played with the dog. 'Just shows you. The difference an animal can make. Reckon he's got a new friend there.'

'I think you may be right,' Anna said, laughing. 'Not often she looks so relaxed and happy.'

They watched, amused, as Jacko scrambled to his feet and ran round and round the farmyard, scattering the hens as he flew, with Gracie running after him, her laughter the most wonderful sound that Anna had heard in a long time.

'Who is she, love?' enquired Jane. 'Funny little thing isn't she? Oh!' She turned to face Anna suddenly, her expression full of interest. 'Is she the new doctor's daughter?'

'Yes, she is. How did you guess?'

'Well,' Jane said with a sigh, 'it's a small village.'

'Oh, don't say that. I've been trying to persuade Connor that no one will be gossiping or unkind about her. Don't tell me I was wrong.'

'People are bound to talk, love,' Jane said. 'Doesn't mean they're being unkind. Just curiosity, that's all. Anyone who might have had something bad to say has been firmly put in their place, now we know what's wrong with her.'

'People know?'

'Oh, yes. It's all around the village. Well, there are other kiddies in her class, don't forget, and they all have parents and grandparents. It doesn't take long to get around.'

'What are people saying?'

'That she has a lot of problems, and that the poor doctor must be worn out trying to cope. There's a lot of sympathy for them both. And...' she hesitated.

'And?'

'And there's a few would like to know where her mother is.' Jane eyed her curiously. 'Where is she?'

'I have no idea,' Anna admitted. 'I get the impression she couldn't cope with Gracie, but other than that, who knows?'

'Poor little mite. So, what are you doing with her today then?'

'Connor—Dr Blake—is ill. I've been taking care of them both, and I thought Gracie could use some fresh air for a change.'

'Oh, right.' Jane was quiet for a moment as they watched Gracie pounce on a wriggling Jacko, who proceeded to yelp in excitement and delight as she tickled him. 'Have you heard from Lee lately?'

'Just last night,' Anna said. She felt a prickle of guilt and tried to ignore it. She had nothing to feel guilty about after all. 'He rang me for a quick chat, but he was on his way out, so it really was quick.'

'Going out again?' Jane tutted. 'Always gadding these days, that one.'

'Well I suppose it's quite a hard job that he's doing, so I expect he's glad to let his hair down at the end of the week,' Anna said, not sure why she felt the need to defend Jane's own son from her.

Maybe it was because of their most recent phone call. She'd had a few harsh words to say to him last night, that was for sure. She hadn't been able to hide her irritation when he confessed he was meeting his friends in the local pub.

'Again? But you're out nearly every night!'

Lee sounded annoyed as he defended himself. 'Well, what if I am? I have to have some fun, don't I? I work very hard. Besides, I'm making a new life down here. I have to make friends, socialise.'

'But you seem to do nothing else!'

'For goodness' sake, what's wrong with you? You've never minded before.' Lee's tone had changed. Clearly, he wasn't impressed that she was making a fuss.

'We're supposed to be saving up for our own place,' she reminded him. 'We can't live with Gary forever, and I don't see how we're going to do that if you're spending all your money out socialising.'

'We're not married yet,' he said, sounding snappy. 'Things will change when you get down here. I'm just making the most of it until that day arrives.'

'Making the most of it? That sounds charming.'

'I'm sorry.' Lee sounded contrite. 'I really didn't mean that. You just put me on edge. Look, the wedding's not far off now. Things will be different when you're here. I'm just bored. I hate being stuck in on my own. When you move in we'll start saving properly. Promise.'

It was funny but that hadn't really consoled her, although she'd made reassuring noises and thought he sounded a lot friendlier when they finally said goodnight.

'We all work,' Jane said. 'You work hard all week too. Don't see you gadding.'

She sounded most disapproving, and Anna felt the need to reassure her.

'It's different for me,' she said.

'Is it? Why?'

Anna wasn't sure, now she came to think of it.

'Oh, well, I expect it will all change when I move down to Kent.'

'Hmm. How are the wedding plans coming along?'

'Everything's sorted,' Anna said airily.

'Really? Bit low key isn't it?'

'Aw, look at that!' Anna was glad of the distraction as Jacko suddenly gave an excited yelp and ran off towards a large stone building at the end of the yard.

'Oh, no you don't,' Jane said, shaking her head. 'Got some pigs in there, at the moment. Litter of piglets arrived last week. I wonder if the little one would like to see them?'

'I'm sure she would,' Anna said eagerly, relieved that

the subject had been changed.

A small part of her wondered why. It was awkward, feeling resentful towards Lee after last night's conversation while in his mother's company, even though Jane seemed to share Anna's opinion that Lee was spending too much time socialising—an opinion that Anna hadn't ever publicly voiced.

She couldn't help feeling uneasy, too, that Lee never mentioned the wedding. It was just two weeks away, and it might as well have been months in the future for all the fuss he made about it.

If people thought she was being low-key over the whole event, Lee was acting as if it had nothing to do with him at all. She supposed, living so far away from it all, it was hard to feel involved or excited about the wedding. So, what was her excuse?

She blinked suddenly as a wail of horror sounded around the farmyard. She realised that Jane had opened the barn door to allow Gracie to see the piglets, and contrary to expectations it hadn't been a good move.

Gracie was clearly distressed, and Jacko was eyeing her with a confused and rather worried expression. As her wailing increased, the dog shot off towards the farmhouse, and Julian appeared looking concerned.

'What the heck's going on? What's up with the lass?'

Anna put her arms around Gracie who struggled free immediately.

'What is it? What's the matter?'

It took some moments before she realised that Gracie couldn't bear the smell of the pigs. Admittedly, it was quite pungent, but Anna had never minded it personally. She was rather fond of pigs, who were intelligent and friendly animals, and it hadn't occurred to her that Gracie wouldn't be able to cope with their odour.

Then again, Connor had recently confessed that even the scent of some flowers was too much for her to deal with, explaining why he'd put the ones she'd purchased in the bin, and apologising yet again.

'Okay, sweetie, we'll go. Come on.'

Placing a hand on Gracie's shoulder she hurried her out of the farmyard, casting an apologetic look at the Twidales.

'I'll pop and see you again,' she called. 'Be over one day next week, and I'll bring you up to date with the wedding plans, okay?'

'That'd be grand, love,' Julian said, nodding.

Jane called. 'You take care now.'

It took quite a while to calm Gracie down again, and for her wailing to cease. They were halfway down the road and heading back towards the village green before her sobs turned to sniffles, and she was calm enough to converse with at last.

'I'm sorry, Gracie,' Anna said gently. 'I didn't think.

It was my fault.'

Gracie said nothing, sniffing a few times, and rubbing her eyes with her sleeve. Eventually, she said, 'I liked that dog.'

Anna smiled. 'I could see that. He was very cute wasn't he? I think he liked you too.'

'How do you know that?'

'Well, the way he rolled over to be tickled by you and ran around so that you could chase him. He seemed to be having a lot of fun playing with you.'

Gracie seemed to be thinking about that for a moment. Eventually, she gave a big sigh and looked up at Anna, her face solemn. 'Maybe he did like me then. I don't know. *People* don't like me do they?'

Anna's heart thudded. 'Of course people like you. Why would you say that?'

'Because I'm different.' She gave a little shrug of the shoulders as she said the words, in a clear, matter-of-fact way, with no emotion evident in her tone.

'Did you make friends at your last school?' Anna asked, not sure she wanted to hear the answer. This little girl was close to breaking her heart.

Gracie considered. 'I did sometimes. But then, they always wanted to play with other people, too, and I don't want that. If they're my friend they should just be my friend.'

'Right.'

Anna didn't know how to answer her. She had such a lot to learn about the way Gracie thought and behaved. She realised she hadn't even begun to scratch the surface.

She also realised, suddenly, that she'd quite like to find out more. Gracie's big brown eyes were so serious, and she looked so earnest about everything. She was such a solemn little girl, and Anna longed to make her feel better, even knowing that there was no way she could work a miracle.

The only thing she could do for Gracie was to be there for her, to try to understand, to be patient, and to care for her. Then she jolted as she remembered that she wouldn't be around to do all those things. Time was ticking on, and she would soon be saying goodbye to Gracie, to Connor, to the entire village. Which reminded her, she thought, sighing inwardly, she needed to call at Spill the Beans and pay the deposit on the wedding cake.

As they crossed over the beck and approached the row of shops, she told Gracie of her plan.

Gracie seemed quite happy to go into the café with her, and as they entered, she sniffed the air quite appreciatively. Evidently, the smell of new bread and freshly brewed coffee was a lot more pleasant to her than the smell of pigs, which wasn't surprising really.

One half of the shop was filled with tables, where a

handful of customers sat eating some delicious-looking scones, cake, and sandwiches. The other half was the bakery, and a glass counter ran the full length of the shop, displaying a selection of very tasty-looking treats.

Anna spoke to Chloe, the assistants at the counter, explaining she was there to pay the deposit on the cake she'd chosen. As she handed over her debit card, Nell, the owner of Spill the Beans, came through from the kitchen at the back. Her face was red from the heat of the ovens, but she had a broad smile on her face.

'Afternoon, Anna. Not long now, eh? Bet you're getting ever so excited.'

Anna tried to sound as if she was agreeing with Nell, without actually doing so. She felt a hypocrite, but how could she tell anyone that the wedding was having little effect on her at all? It was too overshadowed by the imminent move to Kent, away from her home, her friends, and everything that was dear and familiar to her.

Luckily, Nell had spotted Gracie and seemed intent on making a new friend.

'Hello, my love. You're Dr Blake's daughter, aren't you?'

Gracie nodded solemnly, and Nell beamed at her.

'I'm Nell. Very pleased to meet you. Now, what happens when I meet a new member of our little community first time, is they get a free cupcake. So would you like to choose one?'

She indicated the shelves behind the glass counter, and beamed encouragingly at Gracie, who looked a bit hesitant, hovering half behind Anna, and peering round at the cakes, as if not sure whether to agree to this custom or not.

After a few moments, when Anna held her breath and prayed there wouldn't be a scene, Gracie suddenly pointed to a pretty cupcake with lilac icing and little sugar violets on the top.

'That one,' she murmured, almost imperceptibly.

Anna nodded and Nell scooped one up and placed it carefully in a paper bag.

'And for Daddy?' Gracie said.

Anna flushed but Nell grinned.

'Quite right. Can't leave our new doctor out,' she agreed, adding a second cupcake to the bag. 'There you go, little one. Come and see us again won't you? Always got plenty of different cakes to try.'

Gracie nodded, and Anna's heart lifted as she saw the hint of a smile on the little girl's lips.

'Thanks, Nell,' she said gratefully, and Nell winked. Evidently, she'd heard tales of the doctor's daughter too.

Gracie seemed quite contented to head home alongside Anna, clutching her little bag of cakes in her hand, and skipping every now and then. She even laughed as one of the sheep decided to cross the footpath in front of them, forcing them to halt and wait. Clearly, sheep didn't have the negative effect on her that pigs did, which was a good job, considering how many of them wandered freely around the village.

Gracie watched the ewe trot down the road then glanced up at Anna, her brown eyes bright with amusement.

Anna felt a tugging at her heartstrings, and suddenly her own eyes filled with tears. She blinked them away, surprised at herself. Gracie seldom seemed so happy and seeing her like that had really moved Anna.

She realised, suddenly, how fond she was of the little girl already. It was going to be hard to leave her behind.

***

Connor was sound asleep when they got back to Chestnut House. Anna tiptoed upstairs, peered round the bedroom door, and saw him lying in bed, eyes closed, his breathing deep and regular. Smiling to herself, she closed the door gently behind her and went back downstairs to put the kettle on.

Gracie ate her cupcake and watched *Beauty and the Beast*, while Anna drank her cup of tea then tidied the downstairs rooms. She put some washing on, then settled next to Gracie to watch the end of the film, smiling to herself as Gracie sang along to the songs as usual.

Hearing a creaking sound coming from upstairs she glanced at the clock. Almost half past one! Connor must surely be hungry by now.

'I'm going to make your daddy some soup. Would you like some? Or is there anything else you'd prefer?' she asked Gracie.

Gracie thought about it. 'Toast.'

'Toast? You had toast for breakfast. Wouldn't you like something else?'

Gracie folded her arms. 'Toast. That's what I like. That's what I want. I don't want anything else.'

Anna nodded. 'All right, toast it is. And a cup of tea? Or juice?'

'Juice please.'

Anna prepared Gracie's meal, such as it was, then heated some soup and made a cup of tea for Connor, which she placed on a tray.

As Gracie settled with her own tray on her lap, she said, 'Don't forget to take Daddy's cupcake to him.'

Anna nodded and put the bag on the tray. 'Thank you, Gracie. Let's hope he can eat it.'

Connor was awake and struggled to sit up as she walked in.

'You shouldn't have bothered,' he told her, looking distinctly guilty. 'I should be downstairs now, making my own lunch.'

'Don't be silly. How are you feeling?'

He leaned back against the pillows and took a deep breath. 'I feel much better than I did. I'm just so tired, but I suppose that's normal. It will pass. I should feel better each day now.'

'That's great. You had me worried for a while.' She smiled at him and nodded towards the tray. 'I'll just put this on your lap. Tomato soup and a cup of tea. Oh, and there's a cupcake there, courtesy of Nell at the bakery, and chosen especially by Gracie.'

'Gracie chose it?' He looked surprised. 'You mean, she actually made a conversation with this Nell?'

Anna nodded. 'She was absolutely fine. She chose one for herself too, and she thoroughly enjoyed it.' She sat down gingerly on the edge of the bed, careful not to knock the soup. 'I took her to the farm, as I said I would.'

He looked at her, clearly wary. 'And?'

'She was great at first. Totally fell in love with their sheepdog.' She hesitated. 'Then she got wind of the pigs. Hmm. That didn't go down too well at all. She didn't like the smell of them, and it really upset her.'

'Oh no.' He looked stricken. 'How did she react?'

'Got a bit panicky. Just wanted to get away, which was fine. We left the farm straight away.'

He studied his soup. 'I expect the Twidales weren't

too impressed.'

'They understood. They didn't make a fuss about it. They're lovely people. You must stop worrying.'

He didn't reply and she put her hand gently on his shoulder. 'Hey. Stop it. Come on, eat your soup.'

He looked at her for a moment, then picked up his spoon. At first, he didn't seem too keen on the thought of eating anything, but within a few minutes he was devouring his soup hungrily.

'You enjoyed that!' she remarked, grinning at him as he put down his spoon and gave a big sigh.

'Can't believe how hungry I feel all of a sudden,' he admitted. 'I haven't fancied eating anything for ages, but now...'

'Do you think you can manage that cupcake then?' she said, nodding at the bag.

Carefully, he removed the cupcake and stared down at it. 'And Gracie chose this one?'

'She did. She wasn't about to leave you out, that was for sure.'

He smiled. 'Thank you, Anna.'

'For what?'

'For everything you've done for us. Honestly, I'd have been lost without you.'

'It's been a pleasure,' she said, truthfully. 'I've enjoyed myself to be honest. Gracie is lovely.'

'Really?' He studied her face, his eyes burning into

hers. 'Do you really think that?'

'Of course I do.'

They stared at each other for a long moment, and Anna felt her stomach lurch. Even looking so tired and drawn, he was an attractive man. And there was something about his expression that was tying her insides up in knots. She could barely breathe.

Suddenly, his voice, sounding oddly strained, broke the silence. 'How are things at the surgery?'

'What?' She blinked. 'Oh, oh yes, they're fine.' She thought it best not to mention how unhappy patients were about the planned changes. Hopefully, their stream of complaints and protests would make the practice manager rethink, but Connor wasn't up to hearing about all that. 'Just ticking along as usual.'

'Glad to hear it,' Connor said. His eyes met hers again, and he swallowed. 'I don't think I'm quite ready to eat this cupcake yet after all.'

'No, well, never mind. It will keep.' She took it from his hand, feeling a tremor as her skin brushed against his, and placed the cupcake back in the paper bag. 'I'll put it on your bedside table, along with your cup of tea, so if you feel hungry later you know where it is. I'll take this tray down now. Would you like the television on?'

He nodded. 'I think so. I'm not about to go to sleep. At least, not for a while.'

She flicked the television on and handed him the

remote. 'Okay, if you need anything just call me,' she said, noticing his mobile phone sitting beside the mug.

Without thinking, she bent over and kissed him lightly on the cheek. Why on earth had she done that?

Colour flooded her face, and she stood up, not daring to look at him as she headed for the bedroom door.

'Anna?'

She turned, reluctant to meet his eyes, but he was smiling at her and holding out his hand. She took it carefully, hitching the tray under one arm. He squeezed her hand tightly, then let her go, leaning back into his pillows as if suddenly exhausted. She smiled shyly then left the room.

But as she closed the door behind her, her heart thudded, and she felt overwhelmed with guilt and confusion. Something was definitely happening between herself and Connor, and Lee suddenly seemed a million miles away.

Chapter 10

Anna called at the café on the way home from work. It had been a long day, with a steady stream of patients coming in, demanding answers about the future of the surgery—answers she couldn't give them, as much as she'd love to be able to reassure them.

The locum had been quite put out that there was no practice nurse based at the surgery, and that patients only got to see a nurse twice weekly, unless they made the long bus journey to Helmston.

'Ridiculous,' he muttered. 'I really want Mrs Jameson to have an urgent blood test, but she says she can't go to Helmston. Can't manage the journey apparently. Not that she'd be able to get a blood test, anyway. I know for a fact that the nurses are booked up for the next week. Why isn't there a nurse here permanently?'

'You tell me,' Anna said. 'We used to have one, back in the day when there were two doctors based here, but now we're just seen as some backwater that's irrelevant. No wonder they want rid of us.'

'Can the district nurses visit her?' he demanded

irritably.

Anna shook her head. 'They don't visit unless the patient's housebound. Mrs Jameson isn't housebound; she just doesn't like buses. Do you want me to book her in tomorrow morning so you can take the bloods?'

'That's the nurses' job!'

Anna shrugged. 'At Castle Street and plenty of other practices, yes, but here we have to do things a little differently. The bloods must be taken in the morning, obviously, for collection and delivery to the lab, and we don't always have a nurse here. My dad often did the tests himself. He didn't see it as a big deal. It's just the way we do things round here. There are a lot of elderly patients in this village, and they can't all get to Helmston easily. I know it's alien to people used to the modern health service, but my dad was an old-fashioned kind of doctor, and he adapted his methods to suit the situation of the locals.'

'Yes, well, that was very kind of him I'm sure, but it's no long-term solution. It all seems very patchy and unreliable to me.'

Anna's day had just hit rock bottom when Beverley asked to have a private word with her.

'Fact is,' she said, without preamble, 'I'm handing in my notice.'

'Your notice!' Anna couldn't believe it. 'But you've only just started here.'

Beverley looked unconcerned. 'Maybe, but it hasn't taken me long to realise I hate it. It's a boring job, and I've been offered a better one.'

'Really? And where's that?' Anna said.

'The Sailor's Arms, just outside Whitby. Reckon a pub will be a bit more fun than this place. I'm sick of working for doctors. I mean, it's all bad news isn't it? Everyone's ill or old.'

Anna couldn't even bring herself to start on that subject. The woman was a moron.

'You do realise you've completely dropped us in it? You know I'm leaving here soon. I needed someone to take over from me. So how am I going to train someone now, even supposing the manager gets himself into gear and appoints someone else in that time?'

'Well, I'm sorry I'm sure,' Beverley said, not sounding in the slightest bit sorry, 'but I have to put myself first. This isn't the right job for me.'

'No, well,' Anna said with a sigh, 'I can't argue with that.'

So Anna's day had been stressful, and she didn't feel up to cooking when she got back to Chestnut House. Instead, she popped into the café and bought a large meat and potato pie. That would do them all for tea.

Nell put it in a bag then handed her another smaller bag.

'What's this?' Anna raised an eyebrow.

'Cupcake for Gracie,' Nell replied. 'With my very best wishes. Tell her I said hello.'

'Aw, thank you, Nell. That's lovely of you,' Anna said, smiling. 'She'll be delighted.'

'It's the same as the one she chose last time. Wouldn't want to upset her,' Nell said, winking. 'See you later, Anna.'

As Anna pushed open the door to Chestnut House the smell hit her immediately. Something was cooking already. Surely Gracie wasn't attempting to make tea? She hurried into the kitchen and stopped, surprised to see Connor standing by the oven. He was unshaven but dressed, and he smiled as she placed the bakery bags on the worktop.

'What on earth are you doing?' she demanded, noting that he looked rather pale and a bit unsteady on his feet.

'Cooking a pizza,' he said. 'Gracie was hungry and wanted fishfingers, so I made her some and noticed we had this pizza in the freezer. Suddenly I realised I was hungry too, so I put it in the oven. You're welcome to share it if you like? Gracie won't eat it. She doesn't like the way all the toppings are mixed up on it. She thinks it looks messy.' He managed a wry grin.

'I brought you a meat and potato pie,' Anna said faintly. She was quite perturbed at how upset she felt to see him up and about again. Not that she wanted him to be ill, of course, but it would mean she was no longer needed. There would be no reason for her to stay any longer at Chestnut House.

As if he was reading her thoughts he said softly, 'I guess you can go home tonight. I've been downstairs all day today, and I've managed perfectly well.'

'But it's still early days!' She spoke with more force than she'd intended, and blushed. 'I mean, you don't want to tire yourself out do you?'

'I won't do that. I'll take it easy; I promise.' He sank into a chair and looked up at her, his face suddenly serious. 'I really appreciate all you've done for us, Anna. The way you've taken care of Gracie, and—and of me. I can never thank you enough. But, after all, you have your own life to lead, and you must be busy enough preparing for your wedding and your move down to Kent. It's not long now is it? And I expect you have a million things to organise. You must be so excited.'

What was he trying to say to her? That the moments between them had meant nothing? That she had to put all thoughts of him aside and concentrate on her fiancé? Well, he was right wasn't he? So why did she feel so desolate?

'I—I suppose you're right,' she managed. 'I'll get my things now.'

'You don't have to go this minute,' he said. 'If you'd

like to stay and eat first—'

She shook her head. 'No, it's fine. I'll get back to Izzy's. That meat and potato pie will do for your tea tomorrow.' She nodded at the bag. 'Oh, and there's a cupcake there for Gracie.'

As she headed towards the hallway his voice came to her, sounding suddenly brisk and business-like.

'I won't be in at work for the rest of the week, but I'm hoping to be back on Monday. Your last week at the surgery. I can't miss that can I? Exciting times ahead.'

Feeling nauseated she merely nodded and went upstairs to pack. She needed to get away. She needed to think, to talk things over with Izzy. Because everything had changed, and she didn't know what she was going to do about it.

***

'I knew it!' Izzy almost choked on her wine as Anna finally finished telling her what was on her mind. 'I've seen this building for the last couple of weeks, and I just knew you were falling for him.'

'I feel so ashamed,' Anna admitted. 'I hate myself for feeling this way.'

'You can't help how you feel,' Izzy assured her. 'Besides, it's not as if you've acted on it, is it?'

'Of course not!'

Well, apart from that peck on the cheek. But that was because he looked so ill, and she felt so sorry for him. Other than that, she hadn't done anything that Lee could reproach her for, and she never would. But she still felt disloyal. How could this have happened? How could she possibly be so attracted to another man when Lee was her world?

'Do you still love Lee?' Izzy was watching her thoughtfully.

'Of course I do!'

The idea that she didn't love him was unthinkable. He was her companion through life, the one who had always been at her side, ever since they were children. She would never want to hurt him.

'Why would you even have to ask?'

Izzy shook her head slightly. 'Well, come on, Anna, let's be honest. The biggest day of your life is coming up and you've barely shown an interest. This wedding could be someone else's for all the excitement it's given you. I mean, choosing a dress online, and a dress that could be worn any old day at that! And leaving the cake until last minute, and a simple buffet at the local pub. I know, I know,' she said, holding up her hands as Anna started to protest, 'you don't want a big fuss because of your dad. I get that, honestly I do. But I can't help feeling that you're just not that bothered about this wedding because you're not that bothered about being married to Lee.'

'I love Lee!'

'I'm sure you do,' Izzy said, her eyes kind. 'I've never doubted it. But are you in love with him?'

'Is there a difference?'

'You know as well as I do that there's a huge difference. Does Lee make your heart race? Do you long to touch him when you're around him? Do you think about him all the time when he's not there? Does your stomach flutter when he walks into the room?'

Anna clutched her glass in dread. She couldn't, in all honesty, say that Lee had that effect on her at all. But the terrifying thing was, Izzy had just described her reaction to Connor exactly.

So, what did that mean? Was she in love with Connor Blake? And, if so, how could she walk into a registry office with Lee and promise to be his wife? Yet, equally, how could she possibly let Lee down? She had never felt so confused.

'Maybe,' said Izzy, clearly guessing how she felt from her silence, 'you should go and see Lee again? Talk things through with him.'

'And tell him about Connor?' The idea was horrific. She could never hurt him like that.

'I don't think you have a choice,' Izzy said gently. 'You can't go through with the wedding, feeling like this about another man.'

Anna took a sip of wine then shook her head, determinedly. 'This thing with Connor—it's just a silly crush. It's probably last-minute nerves about getting married, moving away. The whole thing has been stressful, and I've latched onto Connor for all the wrong reasons. It will pass. All I have to do is keep a professional distance and it will go away. I'll be over him in a day or two. You'll see.'

'Hmm.' Izzy didn't look convinced, but Anna was suddenly determined to prove her theory correct. She would be an efficient, professional receptionist, and would treat Connor as she would treat any locum doctor working at the surgery. Nothing was going to make her hurt Lee. The wedding would go ahead as planned.

Chapter 11

It was a spur of the moment decision, and Connor regretted it as soon as he'd made it. He'd seen the advertisement in the local paper and wondered if Gracie would be able to cope with it. After all, sitting in a crowded theatre, surrounded by strangers, was hardly the ideal environment for his daughter. Yet, the production of *Chitty Chitty Bang Bang* had received rave reviews, and Gracie got so few treats, and she loved the film version. Maybe it was worth taking a risk?

Having decided that he would do it, he couldn't explain why it was that he purchased three tickets, with the intention of asking Anna to accompany them.

Maybe it was because she was so good with Gracie, and he'd hoped that she would be a help to him if things didn't go as smoothly as he hoped? Or maybe it was that he wanted to thank her for all her hard work, taking care of them both when he was ill? Or was it because she would be leaving in just over a week, and it was his way of saying goodbye?

At the back of his mind, he was very much afraid

that it was none of those things that made him ask her if she'd like to join them, but he refused to acknowledge what was lurking there in the depths of his subconscious. It was too risky, and only likely to bring pain if he examined it too closely.

Anna looked quite shocked to be asked. She'd popped round to Chestnut House a couple of times during the week, just to check things were okay. On the surface, she'd been friendly and concerned, but there was something different about her. She'd seemed rather distant. He supposed it was because she was distracted by her upcoming move. It wasn't long now. A matter of days, really.

'I—I'm not sure,' she'd stuttered, as he showed her the online booking one evening, explaining that the Helmston Players were hardly West End standard, but that the production had been well-received, and he thought Gracie would enjoy it.

'Oh, right.' That threw him. He'd hoped for a bit more enthusiasm. 'It's just—well, I think Gracie would feel more comfortable if we were both there, and to be honest I'm a bit nervous about taking her alone.'

'Are you sure you're up to it? You haven't been out of the house for nearly a fortnight.'

'Well I need to make a start then don't I? I'm back at work on Monday after all.'

She seemed to consider that for a moment, then

nodded. 'Fair enough. Okay, thank you.'

'Wonderful. I'll pick you up around half past six tomorrow night.'

'That would be great. Thanks.'

And so he found himself standing in the foyer of the Helmston Grand Theatre, which wasn't all that grand in truth, but was a pleasant enough provincial theatre. Gracie looked distinctly uncomfortable, eyeing the crowds of people with anxiety. Trying to distract her, he gave her a programme and pointed out the characters to her, hoping the sight of Caractacus Potts and Truly Scrumptious would calm her.

Even so, she looked as if she was about to have a meltdown, and he was relieved when they were allowed into the theatre itself and shown to their seats.

He'd had the foresight to bring the duvet cover with him, which he placed over the burgundy dralon, ensuring Gracie didn't have a screaming reaction to the material. She sat between him and Anna, clutching the programme tightly and staring round with wide eyes, full of fear.

'It will be all right, Gracie,' Anna murmured. 'Ooh look,' she added, pointing at a photograph in the programme, 'there's Jeremy and Jemima.'

'They're not Jeremy and Jemima,' Gracie said, shaking her head. 'And that's not Caractacus. They're different. It's all wrong.'

Connor felt his stomach flip over. She was getting upset because the characters were played by different actors to the ones in the film that she watched frequently. He should have thought of that. She had a certain image in her mind, and she didn't react well when things were changed.

He felt panicky. She was going to start screaming in front of all these people. It would end very badly indeed. Why had he ever thought things would be all right? He'd made a serious error of judgement.

His train of thought was disturbed as the soft tones of Anna's voice floated towards him. She was singing a song from the film—Truly Scrumptious—and Gracie was staring up at her, eyes full of delight.

Within seconds Gracie was singing along with her, and Connor watched them, awestruck. Anna had known exactly what to do to calm the situation. He felt that now all-too-familiar fluttering in his stomach as he watched her, smiling and nodding at Gracie as she continued to sing.

She was so lovely. Pretty, kind, and calm. Her blue eyes were currently shining with enthusiasm, but he had seen them soft with compassion, warm with understanding, and—he mentally shook his head. No, he must have been mistaken there.

He'd thought, once or twice, that he'd seen something else in those eyes. Some spark that he recognised because it reflected something he felt himself. But he must be wrong because she was in love with this Lee chap. About to get married to him, for heaven's sake.

Whatever he felt for Anna, he had to put it to one side, because she wasn't his and she would never be his. In exactly one week she was getting married and moving away. He would never see her again.

He felt a lead weight sitting in his chest, and all the joy seemed to evaporate from him.

'It's starting, it's starting!'

Gracie's voice was full of excitement as the curtain went up, and for the next couple of hours Connor did his best to push all thoughts of the coming separation from Anna away, as he sat beside his daughter, listening to her singing along with the actors onstage, hearing her delighted clapping, holding her hand as she squealed at the dreaded Child Catcher and laughed at the Baron and Baroness. By the end of the show he realised he'd enjoyed it almost as much as his daughter, who was clearly enraptured by the whole thing. Judging by the happy expression on Anna's face, she'd enjoyed herself too.

He knew he should take Anna straight home afterwards. Anything else was only asking for trouble, prolonging the agony, but he couldn't help himself. He found himself asking if she would like to stop by

Chestnut House for a coffee before he took her home, and couldn't deny the thrill he felt when, after a moment's hesitation, she agreed.

Gracie was in a state of bliss—dancing around the living room, singing every song from the play and quoting huge chunks of dialogue. How she remembered it all was beyond him. He couldn't, that was for sure.

'She really loves music doesn't she?' Anna mused, as they wandered into the kitchen and Connor flicked on the kettle. 'You know, you really ought to think about sending her to dance class.'

'Dance class?' He frowned, not sure how he felt about that.

'There's one in Hatton-le-Dale,' she said, referring to the next village. 'It's in the village hall, and it's run by two lovely girls. They've won loads of competitions, and they're so kind and enthusiastic. Lots of local kids go there. I'm sure Gracie would enjoy it.'

He shook his head, handing her a mug of coffee and sitting at the table beside her. 'I doubt she'd fit in. You know what it's like.'

'Sorry, but I think you're wrong.' Anna's tone was appealing. 'Honestly, Connor, I really believe she'd love it, and Faye and Jenna are so good with children. I know they'd be willing to help if there were any problems, and I just think, let Gracie concentrate on her dancing and she'd be in heaven. Plus, she's good at it! Why not let her try?'

He smiled. 'I'll think about it. It's good of you to think of things for her to do. I appreciate it.'

'You really don't get it, do you?' she said, her face suddenly earnest.

'Get it? Get what?'

'You act as if I'm doing you this massive favour all the time. What you don't seem to understand is that I enjoy being around Gracie. I think about her a lot, and I like to make her happy. It makes me happy. She's such a lovely little girl.'

He found he was blinking away tears and took a sip of coffee to hide them.

'Really, Connor, you must have more faith in her. You also need to have more faith in yourself. You're doing a great job. And, as for the villagers—they're not the judgemental monsters you seem to believe. Everyone's so kind, and they've been really understanding about her. Nell sent that cupcake the other day, out of the goodness of her heart. I didn't buy it. You must give people a chance. Faye and Jenna will welcome her with open arms. I can guarantee it.'

'I'm sorry,' he mumbled. 'I know I must come across as thoroughly ungrateful.'

'It's not that,' she said. 'I just want you to feel less stressed. I want you to start enjoying your own life, instead of being permanently on alert.'

'Is that how I seem?'

'Yes.' She grinned. 'Apart from when you had flu. Then you were too exhausted to care. Gracie could have burned the house down and you still wouldn't have shifted from that bed. Poor you. You looked dreadful.'

'I felt it,' he admitted. 'Truth is, Anna, I couldn't have coped without you. Mum was too busy looking after Gran, and I couldn't let her know what was going on here, or she'd have felt completely torn. And we haven't got anyone else.'

'No one?' Anna's face clouded. 'That's so sad. But what about...'

Her voice trailed off, and Connor studied her face, seeing the embarrassment that was clear in her expression.

'What about...?'

'It doesn't matter,' she said quickly. 'Forget it.'

'You were going to say, what about Gracie's mother?' He put down his mug. 'That's right, isn't it?'

He watched a pink flush spread across her cheekbones and thought how pretty she looked. With a huge effort, he dismissed the thought and concentrated on his ex-wife instead.

'Tina lives in Norfolk now. She's married to a man who owns his own market garden, and she's extremely contented. She always was keen on plants and flowers. She's got the ideal life really. For her, at any rate.'

'I'm sorry. I didn't mean to pry.'

'It's not a big secret,' he said with a slight shrug. 'I know Mum acts as if Tina was some evil, heartless woman, but it's not like that. Mum just can't get her head around any mother walking away.'

'But you can?'

He sighed. 'It was obvious from a very young age that there was something different about Gracie. Tina tried to pretend it wasn't happening, but there's only so long you can lie to yourself. It took us years to get a diagnosis. In fact, by the time it was confirmed, Tina had already gone.'

'I'm so sorry.'

'It was for the best. Tina's a good woman, a kind woman, but she really didn't know how to deal with Gracie. To be honest, she made things worse. She tried, but it was breaking her. I didn't want her to leave, but I understood why she had to. In the end, I realised she'd made the right decision, for her and for Gracie.'

'And what about you?' Her voice was gentle, and he realised suddenly that talking about Tina wasn't painful anymore. He wondered when that had happened.

'It took me a little longer to realise it was best for me too, but I got there in the end.'

'And does Gracie see anything of her mother?'

'It's difficult with Tina moving away. They saw each other every month for a while, but Gracie hated going there and Tina dreaded it. We realised that trying to do the right thing isn't always the right thing after all. Gracie doesn't seem to mind. She talks to her mum on the phone sometimes if she wants to. We leave it with her, really.' He sighed. 'She doesn't seem to think about her much. It's such a shame. For both of them.'

Anna reached out and covered his hand with her own.

'I'm so sorry. It must have been awful for you.'

Her voice sounded choked, and he looked down at her hand for a moment, then up at her face. There was that expression in her eyes again. That warmth, that compassion, that understanding. And something else—something that tugged at his emotions, caused his stomach to give that sickening lurch, and propelled him forward suddenly to kiss her.

Vaguely he wondered what he was doing and told himself that he shouldn't. She was getting married. She didn't feel the same way about him. How could she? Yet nothing could prevent his lips from meeting hers, and he wrapped his arms around her, feeling a surge of delight as she responded to his kiss.

Somewhere inside him, he acknowledged the truth. He had fallen in love with this woman, and it could lead to nothing but despair and more heartbreak. He'd already had to say goodbye to one woman he loved, now he would have to say goodbye to another. He had to stop this right now.

Pulling away from her he muttered, 'I'm sorry, Anna. That should never have happened.'

Part of him longed to hear her deny it. He wanted her to tell him that it had to happen, that it was meant to happen, and that she felt the same.

His heart sank as she finally said, 'I know. I'd better go.'

'I'll get Gracie. We'll walk you home.'

'No.' She shook her head, her face red, her eyes not meeting his. 'Honestly, I'll be fine on my own. It's only up the road. Say goodbye to Gracie for me. Goodnight, Connor.'

'Goodnight, Anna.'

She slipped out of the back door into the darkness, and he closed his eyes, knowing that it was too late to protect himself. He was already grieving for her.

Chapter 12

Monday morning was awkward. Connor wasn't sure if it was just him who felt uncomfortable, or if Anna shared his feelings. He should never have kissed her. It had been completely inappropriate. It was probably a good thing that they only had five days left working together. Then on Saturday she would marry her fiancé and leave for Kent, and that would be that. He just had to survive until Friday. Be polite, he told himself. Be professional. Don't make a big deal out of what happened.

Nevertheless, there was a strained atmosphere at the surgery, and he blamed himself entirely for it—at least, at first. Then he discovered the volume of complaints coming in from anxious patients and discovered that Beverley had handed in her notice.

'Why didn't you tell me?' he demanded, heading thankfully into the office after seeing his last patient of the morning. 'Every single patient I've dealt with so far today has bombarded me with questions, and they're worried sick. Has it been like this the whole time I've been off?'

'Well, yes,' Anna admitted. 'They're all scared, understandably. The locum didn't appreciate it.'

'And Beverley's leaving? Is that true?'

Anna was startled. 'How on earth did you know that?'

'Because three of my patients told me. I have to say, I felt a bit stupid that I was the last to know.'

'I'm sorry. I haven't told any of them, so she must have. I didn't want to worry you while you were so unwell. It kind of floored me to be honest.'

He sighed. 'I can understand that. So, what are we going to do about it?'

'I've spoken to the manager. He's going to send Patricia down on Monday.'

'That will please her. She wasn't exactly thrilled to cover you when you were in Kent.'

'I can imagine.' She bit her lip. 'She hates working here when I'm on holiday or ill. Considers it a punishment—like she's been sent into exile or something. Anyway, she's going to cover here until they've got a new receptionist and trained her up.'

'I see. Well, that should be fun, working alongside her.' Connor shook his head. 'I'm dreading next week.'

He hadn't meant to say it out loud, and he certainly hadn't expected her to comment, so he was quite taken aback when she said, quite seriously, 'Are you?'

The tone of her voice and the look in her eyes told him that she wasn't just referring to his professional life.

He looked away, not sure how to respond. It was hardly the time or the place, and besides, he'd told himself he would keep things business-like.

'Where is Beverley anyway?'

'Gone to the café for a quiche for lunch. Connor—' He almost flinched as she reached out and took hold of his hand. '—About the other night.'

'I've apologised for that,' he said, his voice thick with emotion. 'I don't think we need to mention it again do we?'

'But you didn't have to apologise for it,' she burst out. 'I wanted you to kiss me! And we need to talk, don't we?'

He turned back to her, shocked to see the pleading expression in her face. 'Do we? What would be the point?'

'But clearly something's going on. You must have felt it, too! I know you have, or why would you kiss me?'

He removed his hand from hers. 'It was the emotion of the night, after Gracie had had such a good time, and we were so happy and relieved.'

Her face fell. 'Really? Do you mean that?'

'Oh, Anna.' He closed his eyes for a moment,

longing to tell her how he really felt. 'Have you said anything to your fiancé about this?'

When she didn't reply he opened his eyes and surveyed her. She looked guilty, and that told him all he needed to know.

'Not yet,' she murmured. 'I didn't know what to say. I don't know what's happening.'

'What's happening is that you're about to get married to your childhood sweetheart.'

'I know that, but—'

'But what? Anna, this is something you've planned for years. You told me so yourself. And just about every patient at this practice has made it their business to tell me that you and Lee are the perfect couple, meant for each other. I don't want to come between you. I don't want you to walk away from something so solid for—for whatever this is.'

'And what is this?'

'I honestly don't know. Do you?'

She hung her head and he tried to stay calm and level-headed, even though he wanted to tell her that 'this' was something so important to him that, if he could, he'd have got down on both knees right there and then to beg her to stay with him.

But it wasn't fair. Whatever she was feeling for him could be last-minute nerves, the fear of moving away from everything familiar to her. She'd already been through so much lately, losing her father and her home. Maybe latching onto him was like clutching a lifebelt. He couldn't let her throw everything away for that.

'Be honest, Anna. Do you still love Lee?'

She stared at the office wall, as if hoping there was some magical solution pinned to the noticeboard.

'I don't know. Yes. I don't know,' she said wretchedly.

'I think you do,' he replied softly.

'Well, yes, I still love Lee. Of course I do. But this is—different.'

'Because it's not real.' He hated seeing the confusion and pain in her eyes. He couldn't bear to be responsible for it. He took a deep breath. 'The truth is, Anna, you belong with Lee, and you'll make a good life for yourselves in Kent. As for me, I probably won't be here much longer anyway.'

'What?' She stared up at him, anguish in her voice. 'You can't leave!'

'Don't worry. I'm sure you'll find another tenant for Chestnut House easily enough, and I'll give a month's notice of course.'

'I'm not bothered about the house! The village needs you. You can't abandon them now!'

'But it's more than likely that the surgery will close. Let's face facts here. If that happens, I'll need to either move closer to Helmston or find another job. I can't manage working so far from home when I have Gracie to get to school. Besides, let's be honest, we've never really fitted in here have we?'

'Maybe if you'd given everyone a chance you'd realise you could have fitted in just perfectly. But you were too busy keeping everyone at arm's length, too afraid to take the risk.'

'That's probably true,' he admitted. 'Nevertheless, we are where we are. I have to make plans for my future and for my daughter's future, and you need to concentrate on your own life with Lee. I'm right aren't I? Tell me I'm right.'

Please, Anna, he prayed silently, *tell me I'm wrong*.

He watched with a heavy heart as she walked towards the office door.

'I'm going for lunch,' she announced. 'I've printed off your list of visits and the notes you'll need. Beverley should be back in a few minutes if you've any questions.'

The door closed behind her, and it was only then that he realised he'd been holding his breath.

***

'Look, Anna, this can't go on.' Izzy's voice was sympathetic but firm. 'You must sort this out, one way or the other. You're getting married in five days. Five days! And look at you, you're a quivering wreck.'

Anna was about to deny it but discovered she couldn't put the denial into words. Her friend was right after all. The situation was intolerable. She had to do something.

'I don't know what to do,' she confessed. 'It's all such a mess.'

They were sitting in the cosy living room of Rose Cottage. The log fire was crackling in the hearth, and the lamplight made the room even more welcoming and friendly than usual. Yet there was no joy in Anna's heart. She was thoroughly miserable and knew that there was no way a bride-to-be should be feeling this way.

Izzy drew up her knees and hugged them, resting her chin on them as she considered the matter. 'So there's definitely something between you and Connor?'

'I thought so, but now I'm not so sure. He seemed keen to persuade me to go ahead with the wedding, that's for sure.'

'Maybe he just didn't want to be responsible for breaking you up. Let's face it, everyone round here would probably lynch him for it. You and Lee are the perfect couple after all.'

'Oh, don't you start!'

'But you are. Everyone says so, so it must be true. Or do you know differently?'

Anna had a lump in her throat.

Izzy's eyes narrowed. 'Come on, talk to me. What's going on in that head of yours? Have you changed your mind about marrying Lee?'

'I don't know. I can't—I mean, I don't—I just don't know. Lee and me, we've been together for so long. He's almost part of me. But lately it just seems that we never spend any time together, and when we do there's something missing.'

'And that's because of Connor? How you feel about him I mean?'

Anna hesitated. 'I don't think it's anything to do with Connor if I'm being truthful. I mean, all these feelings and doubts were swirling around before I even met Connor. We've had so many years now of Lee being in Kent, studying. It wasn't so bad at first, with him coming home every holiday. And we used to call each other every night, and chat on Facebook. But now he's working he never comes home, and he's always busy so he doesn't have time to call me or talk to me when I call him. It all feels rushed.'

'But if you lived in Kent with him it wouldn't feel like that, would it?'

'Perhaps.' Anna sighed. 'But it's a massive risk to take isn't it? And let's face it, if Dad hadn't died, I might never have agreed to this wedding. It all feels forced somehow. What if I only agreed to get married so quickly because I was lonely, and didn't want to be around to see a new person take my dad's place?'

'Do you think that's what happened?' Izzy asked, surprised.

'If I'm being really honest I dreaded the whole idea of working with another doctor. I couldn't bear the thought of someone else being the village GP. It was Dad's job, Dad's surgery. It felt wrong to continue working as a receptionist for his replacement, so when Lee suggested we get married I jumped at the chance. Maybe it was for all the wrong reasons.'

'But it was Lee's idea, after all, which means he must still love you.'

'I'm sure he does. And I love him.'

'Do you? Really?'

'Of course I do!' Anna could never bring herself to say that she didn't love Lee. The idea was unthinkable. It would have been completely disloyal, and despite everything that had happened between Connor and herself, she couldn't make that final break.

'If Connor hadn't turned up, would you be feeling like this? I mean, I know you said you were having doubts even before he arrived, but were they this bad? Take Connor out of the picture right now and would you still be unsure?'

'I don't have to take him out of the picture,' Anna said gloomily. 'He's taking himself out.'

'What do you mean?'

'I mean, the surgery is almost certain to close, and when it does he's moving. He says it's untenable with Gracie being the way she is. He needs to be able to get to the school quickly and travelling to and from Helmston each day after dropping her off just won't work. Then there's what happens if she's taken ill during the day, I suppose, or if anything upsets her so much they need him to get there quickly. I understand, I really do. But it means, whether Lee and I get married or not, he won't be around either way.'

'Right. Right.' Izzy shook her head, clearly surprised. 'Well, that's a shame.'

'Isn't it!' Anna hadn't meant to sound so bitter and shocked even herself.

'Okay.' Izzy took a deep breath. 'So, Connor's out of the picture. How does it look now? Forget Dr Blake ever existed. Forget Gracie. Forget all that.'

'What? Even the fact that, if I choose to stay, I'll either be unemployed or having to commute to the Castle Street practice every day?'

'Yes, even that. Let's imagine that the surgery has closed, and you're working in Helmston. You're either living back at Chestnut House, or you're renting it out to new tenants, and still living here, whichever you prefer. Connor's gone. You're no longer with Lee. Are you happy? And if not, why not?'

Anna closed her eyes and leaned back in her chair. Izzy had painted a vivid picture, and she put herself right in the centre of it, looking around her, imagining those two possible futures. How did she feel? She experienced a sudden, sickening dread, and opened her eyes.

'Well?' Izzy raised an eyebrow.

'I think I have my answer,' Anna told her. 'I'm going to have to call Castle Street first thing tomorrow. They'll need to send a replacement whether they like it or not. I need to go to Kent.'

Chapter 13

Connor arrived early at work on Tuesday morning. Gracie was extraordinarily calm on the journey to school, even allowing him to hold her hand, and seemed quite eager to get there. He soon found out why.

'Looking forward to our first class no doubt,' Ash Uttridge, Gracie's teacher, explained when he voiced his surprise at her attitude. 'We're putting on a musical for the end of term, and we're learning some of the songs this morning. Casting starts in a week's time, and no doubt Gracie would love to have a main role.'

He thought, with some guilt, that he really ought to warn Mr Uttridge that Gracie might not be around to take part in the musical, so it was pointless to even consider casting her, but he couldn't face going into all that. He had enough on his mind, so he smiled and made appropriate responses, waved goodbye to an incredibly cheery Gracie, and headed to the surgery, his heart thudding the closer he got to it.

Only four more days to go. How was he going to

bear it? It was like some sadistic version of an advent calendar, but instead of counting down to Christmas he was counting down to the day he dreaded more than any other. How could he stand it without Anna? At least in some ways it made the idea of leaving Bramblewick more appealing, despite yet another upheaval.

As he walked he kept his head down, oblivious to the people he passed, and barely registering when a sheep crossed his path. Bramblewick had never really felt like home to him, and he'd always had his doubts about bringing his daughter to such a small place.

At least this way he could say that he'd tried. It wasn't his fault that it hadn't worked out. It was fate. Well, fate and a rather stubborn practice manager.

He tried not to think about the patients who were so worried about the future of the surgery. They would manage. Helmston wasn't that far away. There were buses, after all, and GPs and district nurses would visit those who genuinely couldn't get out to town.

As he pushed open the door of the surgery, he wondered why he was trying so hard to convince himself. He supposed it was because he couldn't stand the guilt otherwise. He had to do what was best for Gracie, and that meant being close enough to get to the school whenever he needed to. He couldn't rely on his mother during term times. It was bad enough that she gave up her own life to be with them during the school holidays. It just seemed such a shame to have to uproot Gracie again, when she was finally showing signs of settling in.

'Good morning! Only four days to go and I'm free.'

Beverley beamed at him, and he wondered how she could be so insensitive. There seemed to be no acknowledgment that she'd caused problems for them, let them down. And she seemed oblivious to the fact that it was also Anna's last week. He almost envied her that.

'So there are. Where's Anna?'

Beverley tutted, clearly annoyed at his lack of interest. 'In reception.'

Connor squared his shoulders and headed through the door into the reception area, where several patients were already sitting chatting to each other, none looking particularly ill. Anna was sitting behind the desk, and she was on the telephone. He heard what she was saying and gripped the door handle, his tension increasing.

'So, that's okay? I'm so grateful. I know I've caused you some hassle, but I just have to do this. Yes, last minute problems with the move I'm afraid. No, it's not the wedding.' He saw her mouth curve into a smile— the mouth that he had so recently, and so foolishly, kissed. 'Oh no, don't worry about that. I'll definitely sort things out, and I'll be back on Friday morning, I promise. Thanks, Pat. You know where everything is and what needs doing? Okay, great. I'll tell Dr Blake, and I'll make sure Beverley's here early to let you in. Bye.'

She replaced the receiver, and he watched as she rubbed her forehead wearily, clearly oblivious to his presence. He felt that he should go back into the office, but he was too slow. She looked up and saw him, her expression changing from weariness to embarrassment.

'Connor! I'm sorry. I should explain—'

'You don't have to. I heard. You're going to Kent for a couple of days. Problems with the move. I'm sorry, I didn't mean to eavesdrop.'

'I need to see Lee,' she said faintly.

Of course she did. She'd be feeling guilty. This wobble, or whatever they wanted to call it, had clearly passed, and now she was cursing herself for her perceived disloyalty. She would want to make it up to her fiancé before he arrived for the wedding. He couldn't blame her for that.

'Please, you don't have to explain,' he said, holding up his hand. 'As long as they're sending someone to cover you it's not a problem.'

'No, but—' She broke off as there was a sudden commotion in the waiting room. 'What on earth?'

'Dr Blake! Can you help please?'

Anna hurried to join him as he rushed to the door, where two elderly people had just stumbled in.

'What is it? What's happened?'

'Mrs Jessop!' Anna gasped. 'Are you okay?'

A woman, probably in her late seventies, was struggling to support another woman of around the same age. Both looked quite pale and shocked, and the lady who was being helped had blood seeping through one leg of her pale blue trousers.

'She fell over, love,' said the uninjured woman. 'Went down like a sack of potatoes. She's cut her knee.'

Anna and Connor helped Mrs Jessop into a chair. 'What happened? Can you remember why you fell? Did you trip?'

'Yes, yes, I must have done. Must have caught my toe on a paving stone or something.'

'She did not,' the other woman said firmly. 'She just dropped. Frightened the life out of me.'

'I'd better check her over. Can you help me get her into my room?'

Anna dashed off to a little room at the side of the reception desk and emerged seconds later pushing a wheelchair. 'Here you go, Mrs Jessop. Sit yourself in here. We'll soon have you sorted.' She called through to the office, 'Beverley, can you take over in reception for a few minutes please?'

'Now then, Mrs Jessop,' Connor said, as they closed

the consulting room door behind them a few minutes later, 'can you tell us exactly what happened?'

'Told you,' said the other woman. 'She went down like a sack of potatoes. I knew she wasn't right.'

'Thank you, Mrs Wainwright,' Anna said, helping the patient roll up her trouser leg, 'but perhaps it would be better if Mrs Jessop told the doctor what she can remember?'

Connor smiled at her gratefully as he washed his hands, then went to the cupboard and took out a dressing pack for the cut on his patient's knee. 'What do you remember, Mrs Jessop?'

'I just felt dizzy,' the old lady admitted, somewhat grudgingly. 'I'd been right as rain. We were sitting there at the bus stop, weren't we, Val? Just watching the kiddies heading off to school and chatting to people as they went by while we waited for the bus.'

She winced as Connor began to clean the cut.

'We're supposed to be going into Helmston.' She smiled suddenly. 'My granddaughter's getting wed. I want to treat myself to a new outfit. Well, it's exciting, isn't it? A wedding, I mean. And me, being grandmother of the bride. Oh, I do love a good wedding.'

Connor's eyes met Anna's, and he looked away quickly. 'This cut's not too deep. It won't need stitching. I'll just put a dressing on it. And then what happened?'

'Well, I spotted Esmé Darnell across the road, looking in Maudie's shop window, and I thought I'd pop across and ask her if she wanted anything bringing back from town. I jumped up and—well, that was it.'

'You said you felt dizzy?'

'Yes. Came on all of a sudden.'

Connor fixed the dressing in place then removed his gloves. Washing his hands again, he said, 'I'm just going to take your blood pressure. Can you take your coat off for me and lie on the examination couch?'

Anna helped Mrs Jessop onto the couch then turned to Connor. 'I'll just pop and tell the other patients there'll be a bit of a delay,' she said. 'Be back in a minute.'

Connor took Mrs Jessop's blood pressure and then got her notes up on screen. Adding her new blood pressure reading in, he quickly scanned through the journal. 'Can you stand up for me, Mrs Jessop? I'd just like to check your blood pressure again.'

'What, while I'm standing up?'

'If you don't mind.'

'But her knee, Doctor!' protested Mrs Wainwright.

'Oh, stop fussing, Valerie. I'm right as rain now.' Mrs Jessop stood, as Connor supported her.

'You're all right? Don't feel dizzy?'

'A bit,' she admitted. 'But I'm okay.'

Connor took her blood pressure again then told her to sit down. 'Your blood pressure's dropped,' he told her.

'What, in a few minutes?' Mrs Wainwright said, sounding surprised.

'You've been on blood pressure medication for a while now,' Connor mused, scanning the notes again. 'But you don't seem to have had it checked recently.'

'No, well, I used to get it checked every six months when Dr Gray was here, but he died just before I was due for my review, and then, what with all the different doctors that kept coming and going, we didn't really get around to booking another one.'

'I see. I'm going to do some blood tests on you, Mrs Jessop, to make sure nothing else is going on, but I think it's your blood pressure we need to keep an eye on. It could be that your medication needs reducing or stopping altogether. Are you okay for me to take some blood now?'

Mrs Jessop sighed. 'You may as well. I don't feel much like going into town now. Sorry, Valerie.'

'Never mind that, Edie. As long as you're all right.'

A few minutes later, Connor was just labelling up the tubes of blood ready to go off to the laboratory, when there was a tap on the door and Anna walked in, carrying a tray with three mugs of tea.

'Thought you could use a nice cuppa to calm your

nerves,' she said, smiling at Mrs Jessop. 'Two sugars for you isn't it? And one for you, Mrs Wainwright?'

'That's right, my lovely. You are good,' Mrs Jessop said fondly. 'Isn't she good, Doctor?'

Connor hoped his face wasn't as red as he suspected it was, judging by the sudden burning sensation around his cheekbones.

'She's an excellent receptionist,' he managed.

'You see?' Mrs Wainwright said. 'What would have happened to poor Edie here if this surgery had closed? How would I have got her to Helmston? And would they have even seen her so quickly?'

'Wouldn't have got a cup of tea, that's for sure,' Mrs Jessop agreed. 'It will be a tragedy if Bramblewick loses its surgery, Dr Blake. Dear old Dr Gray will be turning in his grave. You won't let it happen will you? You are going to fight this?'

'Of course he is,' Mrs Wainwright said confidently. 'Your father certainly would have, wouldn't he Anna? And I'm sure this lovely doctor is made of the same stuff as he was.'

Connor didn't know what to say to that. How could he confess to these two ladies, who were eyeing him so gratefully, and so hopefully, that he wasn't doing anything to save Bramblewick Surgery? That instead, he'd been making plans to move away, start again? That he'd been trying to justify the closure of the branch surgery to himself so that he didn't have to feel guilty?

As Anna handed him a mug of tea, he couldn't meet her eyes. She knew the truth. He felt a wave of shame and tried to push it away. There was nothing he could do. It was out of his hands. It was all out of his hands.

Chapter 14

His mum's voice was cheerful. 'Good morning, love. How are things in Bramblewick?'

Connor's hand tightened on the receiver. That was the million-dollar question, he thought. Where to start?

'Morning, Mum. How's Gran doing?'

'Oh, she's well and truly on the mend.' She laughed. 'You know your gran. Indestructible.'

'Good, good. That's great to hear.'

There was silence for a moment, then her voice broke it, sounding different, sharper. 'What's wrong, Connor?'

'Wrong? Nothing. Why?'

'You can't fool me. I'm your mother. Is it Gracie? Bad time getting her to school this morning?'

'No, no. Actually,' he gave a short laugh, 'she couldn't wait to get there. They've started rehearsals for a musical they're staging at the end of term. She's so excited. She's hoping for a main part of course.'

'Aw, bless her. Well, that's good news isn't it? Do you think she'll get a good role?'

Connor closed his eyes and swallowed hard.

'Thing is, Mum, we might not be here when the play's put on.'

'What do you mean, you might not be there?' She tutted impatiently. 'Come on, Connor. Stop making me play guessing games. What's happened?'

'Truth is, I might be moving back to Sheffield.'

'What? What on earth for?'

'Because the manager and the partners are considering selling off the branch surgery and transferring all patients to the Helmston surgery. If that happens, I'll be too far from school to get there and back comfortably, and I don't think the other GPs will be too happy about me turning up late every day. Besides, Bramblewick's not really my sort of place is it?'

'Don't be ridiculous! It's a lovely little village. Why would you say something like that?'

'Well, all the people at school know about Gracie. Her protests have been heard through the entire village as I've taken her each morning. You know that as well as I do. Then there was that business in the pub. So embarrassing. And Anna took her to the farm one day, and she had to leave because Gracie couldn't stand the smell of the pigs.'

'So what?'

'What do you mean, so what?'

She tutted again, clearly impatient. 'So moving home

is going to make Gracie stop behaving like that is it?'

'Of course not, but it feels different somehow. In a city you can stay anonymous. Here it's like everyone knows you, and they know everything about you. I feel closed in, trapped.'

'That's your problem. No one else gives two hoots about Gracie's behaviour. You're too mired in your own ego, that's your trouble.'

'That's not fair!'

'Oh, isn't it? This isn't about Gracie at all, or what's best for her. This is about you not wanting to attract attention or pity.'

'I don't need pity!'

'And I doubt very much that you're getting any. Honestly, Connor, you ought to thank your lucky stars for what you have. A lovely little house in a beautiful village like Bramblewick, a good job, and a daughter who loves you to bits. All right, life isn't perfect. Whose is?' She was quiet for a moment then added, 'So, did you say Anna took Gracie to the farm?'

Still smarting he replied, 'Yes, she did. And don't go reading anything into that. If you must know, I've been ill. Flu. Anna took care of us while I was incapacitated.'

'Did she indeed? Lovely girl that.'

'Don't start, Mum. She was just being kind.'

'That's because she's a very kind person.'

'I know. I know that.' Didn't he just!

Something in his voice must have given him away because she sounded suddenly eager. 'Has something happened between you?'

He wanted to tell her everything. He wanted to explain how much Anna had come to mean to him, how he longed to be with her, how she was all he could think about day and night, and how much he dreaded her leaving.

Instead he said, 'She's in Rochester right now, visiting her fiancé. They're getting married on Saturday, remember?'

'Oh.' She sounded disappointed. Not half as disappointed as he felt.

Beverley entered his room, not even bothering to knock. She waved a piece of paper at him.

'Visit,' she said cheerily.

'I have to go, Mum. I have a visit to go on,' he said, glad of the excuse to end the call before he gave too much away.

'All right, my love. Give Gracie a big kiss from me and keep me informed of any developments. Such a shame.'

'It's what she wants, Mum,' he said regretfully. 'There's nothing we can do about it.'

She hesitated a moment then said, 'I was talking about the practice closing, Connor. But yes, that's a shame too. We'll talk tonight, young man. No arguments.'

***

The visit was for one Mrs Drake, who lived in a little cottage on the outskirts of the village. After Connor collected his bag and studied the visit request, he glanced up at Beverley, who was leaning back in her chair sipping coffee.

'Not too busy then?'

She cast a shifty look in the direction of the door to the reception.

'Shh, the dragon's in there,' she whispered, referring to Patricia.

Next week, he thought bleakly, she'd be there full time, until they had a new receptionist trained up. Anna would be a married woman and living far away from Bramblewick. She probably wouldn't give the village—or him—a second thought.

'Mrs Drake—does she want anything bringing in?'

Beverley's eyebrows shot up in surprise. 'Bringing in?'

'You know,' he said impatiently, 'from Maudie's? Bread, milk, anything? It says here she's got a leg ulcer, and she's some distance from the shops.'

When she continued to look at him blankly, he sighed. 'Can you ring her and find out?'

'Yeah, yeah sure.'

Beverley put down her coffee and dialled Mrs Drake's home number. After a short conversation, it transpired that Mrs Drake would be ever so grateful if that nice doctor could bring her some teabags from Maudie's and a curd cheesecake from Nell's café. She hadn't liked to ask before, because of him not being Dr Gray, but since he was offering...

It was only when Connor arrived at Maudie's shop that he realised what he'd done. Bramblewick must be having some sort of weird effect on him he thought. He was absorbing their strange ways, like osmosis.

Maudie was all smiles as she handed him the teabags. 'Those are the ones she likes, Doctor. Tell you what, take her these from me, will you,' she added, passing him a bag of sherbet lemons. 'Loves these. Such a shame her leg's playing up again, bless her. Give her my love, won't you? See you tomorrow.'

No doubt she would, he thought. There was always some patient wanting something. He realised he was grinning and straightened his face as he headed towards the café, which was charmingly named Spill the Beans. Nell, a bubbly blonde with big blue eyes, gave him a huge grin as he entered the shop.

'What can I do for you, Doctor?'

'Er, a curd cheesecake for Mrs Drake, please.'

'No problem.' She carefully wrapped one up,

humming softly to herself as she did so. Connor looked around, wondering why he'd never been in this place before. It was a lovely little café. Quite charming. He should bring Gracie in one day.

'There you go, Doctor,' she said, cheerfully, handing him two paper bags. 'There's one of my cupcakes in there, too, for Gracie.'

'I'm sorry?'

'Cupcakes. One of the ones with swirly lilac icing and little sugar violets sprinkled on top. She loves them, apparently. Chose one for you too. Didn't you get it?' She winked. 'Did the little monkey eat them both? Or perhaps Anna snaffled yours.'

'Oh, no, I remember,' he said. 'Of course. Thank you so much. It was delicious. I'll pass this onto her. Very kind of you.'

'No problem. Bless her, she's a little cherub. See you later, Doc. Give my love to Mrs Drake.'

'Yes, yes, I will,' Connor said.

Mrs Drake was in remarkably good spirits when he reached her home, Cuckoo Nest Cottage, and she was full of gratitude that he'd done some shopping for her.

'What a good lad you are,' she told him. 'Just like Dr Gray. Cut from the same cloth, obviously.'

He wasn't sure about that, but it was a nice compliment, given how much esteem his predecessor was held in in this village. After examining and dressing

Mrs Drake's leg, he washed his hands and prepared to leave. The door was pushed open suddenly, and a rosy-cheeked brunette, probably in her late twenties, entered the cottage.

'Afternoon, Doctor. How's our Lulu doing then?' she said, nodding at the patient.

'Lulu?'

'Always calls me that,' Mrs Drake said, laughing. 'My names Louisa, but I've always been Lulu to her, haven't I, Holly?'

'Always. Lived next door to each other since I was born,' Holly explained. 'I couldn't pronounce Louisa, apparently, when I was little, and Lulu just stuck. How's her leg?'

'My leg's just fine,' Mrs Drake assured her. 'Stop mithering and stick the kettle on. I'm sure Dr Blake would appreciate a nice cup of tea.'

'Oh no, really. There's no need to go to any trouble on my account,' Connor assured them, as Holly picked up the kettle and began to fill it with water.

'No trouble, Doctor. Glad of a cup of tea myself. Just got back from Helmston. Proper palaver that is, getting the bus. It's all right for those who can drive, but we're not all so fortunate, and half the time the buses are late. Proper annoying it is.'

Mrs Drake sighed. 'Aye, it's not the best service in the world is it?

'You can say that again. We can't all afford to keep a car, but oh, I do hate going to town on a bus.'

'We'll all be having to do that soon enough, if this hare-brained scheme of the Castle Street lot goes ahead,' Mrs Drake said, shaking her head. 'Proper catastrophe that will be.'

'You're not wrong there.' Holly poured out three cups of tea and handed them round. 'Mind you, we weren't surprised, were we, Lulu?'

'Not really,' she admitted.

Connor cradled his cup of tea in his hands and looked at them questioningly. 'You weren't?'

They both shook their heads. 'Let it run down over the last few years. Used to be two doctors here, didn't there, Holly?'

'Yep, and a nurse. Then Dr Pennington-Rhys left, and it was just Dr Gray. We were expecting a replacement, but none came. Then the nurse's clinics were cut back to twice a week, and she was based at Castle Street. Shocking. Absolute disgrace.'

'Maybe if Dr Pennington-Rhys had stayed things might be different,' Mrs Drake said with a sigh. 'Couldn't blame him for leaving though. After what happened.'

'Oh? What happened?' Connor's curiosity was aroused. He was turning into a gossipy villager himself, he thought.

'His baby girl died,' Holly informed him in hushed tones. 'Cot death. Such a shame. Pretty little thing she was, remember, Lulu?'

'Oh I do. And they were so proud of her, weren't they? Absolutely broke their hearts. Well, it did more than that. It broke their marriage too. She moved away and then, not long after, he went off to work at Castle Street too. Terrible shame. And that's when it all started to change here. Sad story.'

Connor sipped his tea, thinking about the poor couple whose child had been lost so tragically. He couldn't imagine how anyone would ever get over something so horrific. He thought about Gracie and realised how lucky he was to have her in his life. He remembered the cupcake in his bag and smiled. She would enjoy that later, and she would no doubt spend the evening singing the songs she had learned at school for the play.

The play. She would be devastated that she couldn't take part in it.

'Something should be done about all this,' Holly said firmly. 'These bosses need to understand that they're ruining people's lives. It's bad enough for me going all the way to Helmston on the bus, but at least I can walk without difficulty or pain. Not everyone's that lucky. It's a disgrace.'

'Are you going to do something about it, Doctor?'

Mrs Drake leaned forward, her face earnest.

'I'm not sure there's anything I *can* do,' he admitted, feeling ashamed. 'I'm not a partner, you see. Not yet anyway. I don't really have a say.'

'But your opinion must count for something?' she persisted. 'Surely, if you tell them what it's like, how much we rely on the place?'

'We should get up a petition,' Holly decided. 'Get all the villagers to protest. That's what we'll do. What do you think, Doctor?'

'Well, yes, I think you should,' he agreed. 'Your voices should be heard.'

'They won't take any notice of us,' Mrs Drake said sadly. 'We don't matter, obviously.'

'We have to try,' Holly said. 'That's right, isn't it, Doctor? I mean, you have to fight for what you want, don't you? You can't just give up. Bramblewick matters to us all, and the surgery is a vital part of the village. I, for one, am not going to just let it go without fighting.'

Connor stood up. 'Thank you for the tea. It was lovely. I'll be in touch with the district nurses about your leg, Mrs Drake, but don't hesitate to call the surgery if you feel you need to speak to me.'

'Thank you, Doctor.'

They were all smiles as he headed towards the door.

'And you'll back us up?' Holly added. 'If we get up a petition I mean?'

He hesitated then nodded. 'Of course! Of course I'll back you up.'

They beamed at him, and he walked over to his car, thinking a petition wouldn't sway the partners and the manager. It would take far more than that for them to change their minds.

He pulled over near the shops on his way back to the surgery, suddenly realising he hadn't had lunch and he was starving. He'd get one of the pasties he'd spotted in Nell's café. That would fill the gap until teatime at any rate.

As he stepped out of his car he heard someone calling for him, and spotted a man standing outside The Bay Horse, sweeping brush in hand.

'Can I help? It's Ernie isn't it?'

Ernie beamed at him. 'Afternoon, Doctor. Just saw you getting out of your car and that reminded me. What happened in here when you came for your tea—'

Connor flushed. 'I'm sorry about that. My daughter—'

'Oh, you don't have to apologise. That's not why I called you over,' Ernie assured him. 'I know all about your little girl. One of my granddaughters is in the same class, and then Anna explained about the material on the seats, and the noise.'

'Did she?' Connor frowned. 'Then what...?'

'I felt proper bad for you, not being made to feel

welcome. Don't want anyone thinking they can't come in here and enjoy a nice meal. I was thinking, if you have a spare cloth for your daughter, you could leave it here so it's always ready for her whenever you want to pop in for something to eat. And also,' he added, as Connor started to protest, 'I was thinking that you'd be better off coming in through the snug and sitting in the back of the dining area. We have a separate part, all blocked off, see. It's a big table—seats about twelve—and we use it for birthday meals and special events, like. But it wouldn't be a bother for you to have it most nights. It's not often booked out, and as long as you checked first... Little one wouldn't be able to see the other diners, and it's quieter. More private, like. Reckon you could all eat there in perfect harmony. What do you think?'

Connor was stunned. 'That's really kind of you.'

'Not at all. Like to keep my clients happy,' Ernie assured him. 'Now, next time you come in there'll be a drink on the house for you, and for the little one. Look forward to seeing you.'

Connor nodded. 'Thank you,' he said, dazedly. 'I really appreciate that.'

Ernie grinned, and Connor headed to the bakery. What a day it had turned out to be. He couldn't believe how kind and thoughtful everyone had been. Not a bad word or a sarcastic comment about Gracie. Nothing

but understanding and generosity.
   How had he got it so wrong?

Chapter 15

Lee was clearly astonished to see Anna outside the flat when he arrived home from work that Wednesday evening.

'Hello, you. What on earth are you doing here?'

'I needed to see you, Lee.'

Anna stared at him, absorbing every detail of the face that was so familiar and so dear to her. Those warm hazel eyes, that fine brown hair, that gentle smile. She remembered the way his eyes crinkled in the corners when he was amused, and the sound of his laughter. She loved him so much. He was her best friend, her first love. But it wasn't enough. Not anymore.

Gary thought it very amusing to see her at first.

'He's going to Bramblewick on Friday! Crikey, you really are keen, aren't you? Couldn't wait, eh?'

Her face evidently told him that she wasn't in the mood for jokes, and he made his excuses and left them alone in the flat.

Sitting side by side on the sofa, they looked at each

other awkwardly. Anna didn't know where to begin. All the way down to Rochester on the train she'd been rehearsing this speech. It had seemed simple enough, but now, looking at Lee's puzzled face, she didn't know that she could bring herself to do it. What was she thinking? How could she possibly hurt this wonderful man?

Because he was wonderful, there was no denying it. He was the last person she wanted to hurt, yet here she was. She'd travelled all the way from Yorkshire with the sole intention of giving him the news that would break his heart. She lowered her gaze, unable to even look at him anymore, as her shame burned through her.

'So, what's this about?' Lee said, as the clock ticked on, and the uncomfortable silence evidently proved too much for him to stand a moment longer. 'I'm guessing this isn't a social call? Has something happened? Everyone's okay?'

'Oh yes, yes, everyone's fine. I saw your mum and dad the other day. Went to the farm.'

She didn't mention Gracie, but he seemed to know all about it.

'Yes, I know. Mum told me. Said the new doctor's daughter was very taken with our Jacko.'

Anna's skin scorched. 'She was. He was so sweet with her.'

'Haven't seen him for ages,' he said with a sigh. 'I

guess I've missed out on a lot that's been happening back in Bramblewick. It feels like another life somehow.'

Anna stared at him miserably. 'I suppose it does. Whereas, to me, it feels like real life, and this place seems alien and strange.'

Lee watched her for a moment, his eyes narrowed.

'Anna, is this you trying to tell me you're having second thoughts?'

'Second thoughts?'

'About moving here after the wedding? I know it must seem odd to you, but I love it here. My friends, my job. I know you've lived in Bramblewick all your life, but you'd get used to it, you know.'

'I—I'm sure I would eventually.'

She swallowed. She had to be brave.

'But the thing is, Lee, I'm not sure I want to get used to it.'

'Ah.' He stood up, pacing round the flat as he considered her words. 'Is that why you're here? To persuade me to move back to Yorkshire?'

She stared up at him, stricken. He just wasn't getting it, and she was going to have to say the words she didn't want to utter. There was obviously no way round it.

'Lee, I—I think we should call off the wedding.'

He stopped pacing and his eyes pierced into her.

'Call it off? Are you serious?' He sat down beside her

again and took hold of her hands, squeezing them gently. 'You're saying you don't want to get married?'

She took a deep breath. 'I don't think I'm ready to do this. I really don't.'

He nodded. 'I understand. It's been a heck of a year for you, what with your dad dying and having to rent out the house. Moving here, getting married, it's all too much. Look, I get it. If you want to postpone for a while, that's fine. We can do this a few months down the line. Next year even.'

She wasn't being fair to him, and she knew it.

'Lee, stop! That's not what I'm saying. This is so difficult.'

'Why don't you just tell me what's on your mind?' he asked. 'You've always been able to talk to me before. What's changed?'

What had changed? Everything. Anna felt tears swimming in her eyes.

'I'm so sorry. I just think we've had so much time apart, and our lives have gone in different directions. The truth is, I don't want to leave Bramblewick, and I don't want you to leave Rochester. I understand how much you love it here. I know you've got a job you're enjoying, and a great social life, and that's fine. But it's not for me. And I just think, I just think...'

'That maybe we've grown apart?' he said gently.

She blinked the tears away, focusing on his face

which was full of understanding. 'You think so too?'

He hesitated then nodded.

'The truth is, Anna, I feel the same. You and I have been together so long—since we were children. But we've never really lived. Coming down here, I felt differently about so many things. There are so many things I want to do, and I just don't feel ready for marriage or settling down.'

'Then why did you ask me?'

'Because you were in a bad place—emotionally I mean. I felt you needed me to step up, and I thought we could make it work. We love each other, don't we? I thought that would be enough.'

She nodded. 'You always were too kind.'

'It wasn't pity,' he said quickly. 'Honestly, I thought we could be happy together. I still think we could, but...'

'But it's not enough?' she said.

When he didn't answer, she took a deep breath. Her turn to be honest.

'The thing is, Lee, I've met someone. Nothing's happened!' she assured him quickly, as he reared back, clearly wounded. 'I would never do that to you. But, truthfully, I think something could have happened quite easily, if it wasn't for the fact that I'm engaged to you. It feels different. I can't explain, but...'

'But he makes your heart pound, and I don't?' Lee smiled ruefully as her eyes widened. 'I understand more than you realise.'

'You haven't?' Her stomach churned at the thought of Lee being unfaithful to her.

He shook his head. 'Don't be daft. I'd never do that to you. But there have been moments when I was tempted, and that's when I began to think that, perhaps what you and I have—as lovely as it is—just isn't enough. I think that, although I love you so much, and I know you love me, perhaps we're not actually in love with each other. And that's what we want, isn't it? To be in love? I don't know. You're my best friend, Anna, but I suppose there has to be something else in a marriage. A spark that we just don't seem to have. I'm sorry, I don't mean to hurt you.'

'I know that. Just difficult to hear you say it, even though I agree.' She smiled weakly at him.

It was painful to hear Lee admit that he wasn't in love with her, even though she knew he was right to be honest about it. And she had to admit, she felt the same way about him. Best friends they may be, but that didn't make them right for each other. She was glad, despite the pain, that he wasn't trying to persuade her to change her mind. She'd been right to come down to Rochester to confront him. Imagine if she hadn't. What would their marriage have been like?

'We'll always be friends though?' He squeezed her hands again, and she smiled.

'Always.'

'And this new man—the one who makes your heart pound—do I know him?'

She shook her head. 'No. He's the new doctor,' she admitted.

'Ah, the father of the little girl who fell for Jacko. And he's not married?'

'No, of course not. Divorced. Long story.'

'And none of my business. Well, at least you can tell him you're free now. That should make him happy.'

She bit her lip. 'It's not that simple. I really don't know how he feels about me. Besides, it looks as if he'll be moving away from Bramblewick. The surgery might be closing for good.'

'What? Since when?'

'Latest bright idea from the Castle Street practice. They want to sell off the building and transfer all our patients there.'

'But that's crazy! It will never work.'

'I know that. Anyway, if it goes ahead, Connor will be moving away, either to Helmston, or more likely back to Sheffield. He'll probably want to be nearer his mother again, so she can help look after Gracie. I'm not sure he feels this experiment living in the countryside has worked.'

'Experiment?'

Anna explained about Gracie, and he listened

sympathetically, nodding every now and then.

When she'd finished, he said, 'Well, I can kind of understand why he'd need to move then. It would be impossible for him going backwards and forwards to Helmston when he has to settle her in at school and be on hand if she needs him. But hey, Helmston's not too far, is it? And even if he decides to go back to Sheffield, does it matter?'

Anna frowned. 'You mean, go with him?'

He laughed. 'I know, I know. Mad idea! As if you could ever leave Bramblewick behind.' His face turned serious suddenly. 'That was always part of the problem between us, wasn't it?'

She nodded. 'I suppose it was. I just couldn't imagine moving here.'

'But, Anna, our relationship wasn't enough to make you want to leave your home behind. What about Connor? Is he enough for you? Does he matter enough to make you give up Bramblewick and move away?'

Anna leaned back on the sofa, her mind whirling. Move away from the village? Go somewhere new and start all over again with Connor?

Lee patted her arm. 'I'll make you a drink. I think you have a lot of thinking to do.'

Chapter 16

Gracie was full of excitement when Connor collected her from the after-school club that Wednesday evening. He soon found out why.

'Mr Uttridge asked me to sing a song, all by myself, and when I'd finished he clapped and clapped for ages, and he said I definitely had to be in the running for a big part in the play. I want to be Alice.'

'Alice?'

'Yes. She's different to everyone else, like me. All the others understand things and she doesn't. But she's quite clever, and she always keeps trying. In the end it's just a dream you know.'

'So, it's a musical version of *Alice in Wonderland*?'

'Sort of. But it's not like my book. There are some different things in, and some things taken out, and some funny songs. Mr Uttridge said I had a beautiful voice, and he said I was very clever to remember all the words so quickly.'

'Well, he's right about both things,' Connor said, smiling. Clearly, Mr Uttridge was living up to his reputation, and he hadn't seen Gracie this happy for a long time.

As Gracie settled in front of the television, happily eating her evening meal, he sipped his tea, his mind racing. So much had happened during the day that he no longer knew which way was up. Everything he'd thought and believed about this village had been turned on its head.

So many people had proved to him that Gracie mattered to them, and he'd never before experienced a community like Bramblewick.

But he would be moving away soon, and what if Gracie didn't settle? What if her new teacher didn't understand her, the way Mr Uttridge clearly did? What if there was no bakery that sold cupcakes with lilac icing and little sugar violets on them? What if, what if, what if?

Suddenly decided he put down his cup, his mouth set with determination. It was time to make some changes. He had to take charge of his own life, and he knew exactly where to start.

***

'I think you're mad,' Patricia told Connor, as they sipped coffee in his consulting room the next morning.

Connor had wanted to explain his idea well out of Beverley's earshot. Not that he supposed it mattered much. Beverley was leaving the next day after all. She probably wouldn't care one way or the other what happened to the practice. Then again, he wouldn't put it past her to start telling the patients his plans, and he didn't want to give them false hope.

'But I also think you're right if it helps.'

'You do?' Connor was surprised. Patricia had always worked at the Castle Street Practice, so he hadn't expected her to feel any loyalty, or even any interest, in the future of Bramblewick Surgery.

'Used to be a nice little place this,' she told him. 'And our patients really appreciated it. The last few years, since it's been down to one doctor and a part time nurse, more people from this village and the surrounding ones have moved over to Castle Street. We're full to bursting, and it's not exactly convenient for them is it? I think your idea is much better.'

'Then why do you think I'm mad?'

'Because it's such a huge responsibility. Mind you, if I were you, I'd have a word with Dr MacDonald.'

'Oh?'

'He's come from a rural practice himself, and he understands these things. I think he'd be interested, and he's probably your best bet if you're serious.'

'I'm completely serious,' he told her. 'I can't believe it myself, but I've made up my mind now, and nothing's going to shift me.'

She grinned. 'Well, I wish you luck. They can be a stubborn lot you know. I think you'll need all the luck you can get.'

He pulled a face. 'Thanks. I feel so much more confident now.'

'We can but try,' she said, standing up and taking his empty cup from his hand. 'By the way, I've brought a card in for Anna. Everyone at Castle Street has signed it. It's in my top drawer if you want to write on it.'

'A wedding card?' His stomach turned over at the thought.

She tutted. 'Well, it's not Christmas is it?' She sighed. 'Can't believe she'll be Mrs Twidale in just two days. It's not going to be the same without Anna, whatever happens. She would have been welcomed at Castle Street if they did go ahead with the closure you know. She knows the job backwards after all.'

'Yes. She's extremely competent.'

'Ah well, that's the way it goes. She'll have no trouble getting another job. They'll give her a brilliant reference no doubt.' She headed towards the door. 'Don't forget to sign that card.'

'I'll remember. Thanks.'

His heart sank. How could he possibly sign a congratulations card for Anna and Lee Twidale? What was he supposed to write on it?

Nothing that he wanted to write, that was for sure,

not unless he wanted to give himself away, and it was far too late for that. All the joy and optimism he'd been feeling that morning had just fizzled away. The day seemed suddenly bleak, the future pointless.

He turned on his computer, angry at himself. He had a job to do, and it was time to get on with the day's work.

Connor bought chocolates and a good luck card for Beverley during his lunch break and gave them to her in the office before afternoon surgery started. She was quite obviously touched by the gesture and went so far as to give him a hug, which startled him a little.

After heading back to his consulting room, he logged onto the computer and stared at the screen, his mind going over and over the problems he was facing. He'd emailed Riley MacDonald, explaining his thoughts on Bramblewick Surgery, and he'd responded, confirming his interest, and adding that he would like to meet up with him to discuss the situation in full, which sounded promising.

If he could get him onside they could approach the other partners and the manager together. Maybe Riley would be able to get another partner to join them, which would be even better. There was hope at any rate.

As for his other problem… He sighed and rubbed his forehead wearily. There was absolutely nothing he could do about that. Anna had made her choice. He could only wish her well. Which reminded him. He stood, albeit reluctantly. He'd better sign that wretched card, although what he was going to write he had no idea.

As he reached for the door handle he stayed his hand as a knock came from the other side. The door was slowly pushed open, and his mouth dropped open in shock as Anna peered round. She seemed quite startled to see him so close, and that familiar pink flush spread across her cheeks.

He swallowed. 'You're back. I wasn't expecting you until tomorrow.'

They stared at each other for a moment, then she said hesitantly, 'May I come in?'

It was his turn to blush. 'Of course, sorry. Sit down.'

He returned to his seat and fiddled nervously with his computer mouse. His mouth felt dry, and he could feel his heart thumping inside his chest. Casting a sideways glance at her, he saw the flush of pink had receded and she looked rather pale. In fact, she looked quite ill.

Concern overrode all other thoughts, and he turned to face her fully.

'Are you all right, Anna? You don't look well.'

'I've been travelling since early this morning. I'm a bit tired. Besides, it's been a weird couple of days,' she admitted, looking up and meeting his gaze at last.

'Really? For me, too,' he said, with some feeling.

Weird? It had been life-changing, really. He could hardly believe it himself.

'How is Lee?'

He had to ask, and he forced himself to sound casual. It wasn't her fiancé's fault, after all, that he'd gone and fallen in love with Anna. He was the one in the wrong, not this Twidale chap.

'Lee's fine,' she told him. 'Really happy. He loves his job, and he's very happy in Rochester.'

He made himself smile.

'That's great,' he said, tapping a pen on his mouse mat. He couldn't seem to keep still. He felt too wired, too nervous. Annoyed with himself, he put the pen down and tried to sound calm. 'It's a good feeling when you find somewhere that feels like home. Somewhere you never want to leave.'

She looked at him, her eyes stricken.

'But sometimes you have to leave. I mean, it may not be ideal, but if, say, you love someone with all your heart and soul, and they don't belong in the place you love, well then, you have to make a choice. And people matter more, don't they?'

He stared blindly at his monitor. Why was she saying this? He understood already. She loved Lee, and Lee belonged in Rochester. He got it. Why was she rubbing it in?'

'I suppose so.'

'I mean, when you're in love with someone,' she continued, her voice earnest, 'you can be happy wherever you go, as long as they're beside you, can't you?'

Was she being deliberately cruel? 'I'm sure you can.'

'I think so, too,' she said, decisively. 'I love this village so much, Connor, I really do. But I have to follow my heart. When you realise how much you love someone, you must go where they go, and you have to believe that you'll be happy just because they'll be happy. And I think I can be happy, because I'm so in love, and I didn't realise how much before, but now I—'

'For God's sake, Anna!' He couldn't stand any more of it. It was unbearable. 'What are you trying to do to me?'

'I'm sorry?'

'I understand, okay? I get it. You don't have to keep going on about it. You love Lee. Lee belongs in Rochester. You're moving to Rochester to make him happy. What do you want me to say?'

Tears were spilling down her cheeks and he realised suddenly that his own face was wet. Oh, good grief! He rubbed them away, wishing she'd never come back. Why couldn't she just stay away? Do him a favour and get married without him having to set eyes on her. He couldn't cope with all this.

'What did you say?' As her garbled words permeated his conscious mind he lifted his face and stared at her in shock.

She was half laughing. 'I said it's not Lee I'm in love with. It's you. I went to Rochester to tell Lee. To explain. The wedding's off.'

'But—but you and Lee have been together forever!'

'Yes, but when I met you, I realised I wasn't *in* love with him. Oh, I love him, and I always will. He's my best friend. But he doesn't make me feel the way you make me feel, Connor. He never has.'

Her hand moved across the desk to lie beside his own, but he couldn't bring himself to touch her. Not yet. He had to be clear. Make absolutely certain he wasn't misunderstanding her.

'But what did Lee say?'

'He felt the same. We both agreed that this was a childhood romance that just isn't a strong enough basis for marriage.'

'Then, then, are you saying...?'

He couldn't put it into words, too afraid that he'd got it all wrong, but she laughed and, standing, she pulled him to his feet, telling him she loved him and only wanted to be with him, until he finally allowed himself to kiss her with all the longing and passion he'd tried so hard to suppress all those weeks.

As they eventually pulled apart he said, rather dazed, 'Then what was all that talk about moving away? About being happy away from the village?'

Her face took on a serious expression. 'I understand about you having to move away. I really do. And the thing is, as much as I love this village, I want to be with you and Gracie. Wherever you go, I'll go too. I really don't mind.'

He grinned at her, his expression knowing. 'You really don't mind? Honestly?'

She blushed. 'Well, I admit, I do mind a bit. But the difference is, where I was dreading moving away to be with Lee, I'm happy to move away to be with you. I'd far rather lose this place than lose you. And when I realised that, that's when I knew for certain how much I loved you.'

'Oh, Anna.' He shook his head, smiling broadly. 'I have so much to tell you. If things go my way you won't have to move away from here at all. Neither of us will.'

She stepped back, looking up at him in surprise. 'What do you mean?'

'You're not the only one who's done a lot of thinking these past few days. So much has happened to me.'

'Oh? Like what?'

'Like realising I've been a bit of an idiot. All those things you said about me. You were right. I was thinking of myself. I was so afraid that Gracie and I would be judged that I didn't let anyone in, didn't give them a chance. Well, luckily the people of this village weren't going to give up on me, or on Gracie. They seemed to conspire yesterday to prove to me that they're good, caring people, and that this village is the right place for us. Gracie's happy here. I'd be stupid to give up on it without a fight.'

Her eyes were shining with excitement. 'I'm so glad! But what can you do?'

'I'm going to make the other GPs listen. The villagers are getting a petition up, and I'll sign it too, then I'll present it to the partners and make sure they understand the effects the decision to close would have on this community. I've got one of the other doctors on my side already. We may be able to persuade the others. If all else fails, I may be able to buy them out.'

'What?'

'I was going to buy into the business anyway if things worked out here. This way I'll be simply buying the Bramblewick part, instead of into the whole thing. If I can get Dr MacDonald to go in with me, and maybe even find a third partner, we could really make this work. Three GPs based here, and at least one or two full-time nurses. Imagine it! We could attract far more patients from the local villages. I'm sure there'd be plenty who'd rather come to Bramblewick than trail up to Helmston. Don't you agree?'

'I do agree!' she said, laughing. 'Oh, Connor, are you really serious?'

'I'm very serious,' he told her. 'This place is my home now, and it's Gracie's home. I don't want to leave. I don't want to start all over again. I want to stay here, make friends, build a life. I want Gracie to settle. I want to be with you, and I want you to be happy too.'

He kissed her again, gently, then surveyed her with worried eyes. 'I can't make any promises, though, Anna. About this place, I mean. I'm going to do my absolute best, but it may be a challenge. We'll have a lot of work and a lot of persuading to do, and we may not succeed. Then there's Gracie. You know that life with her isn't easy. She's my daughter, and I love her with all my heart, but I know how difficult it can be to live with her. It can be wonderful and fun and rewarding, but it can be exhausting and frustrating and upsetting too. Are you prepared for that?'

She put her hands on his shoulders and gazed steadily into his eyes.

'For as long as I can remember I've taken the safe option. Stayed in this village, worked for my father, lived in the family home, got engaged to my childhood sweetheart. Maybe it's time I took on a challenge or two. And saving this place and loving Gracie—hopefully making a difference to her life—will be worth it.' She smiled at him. 'Anything worth having is worth fighting for. I'm ready to fight.'

Connor pulled her into his arms and closed his eyes. The last few years had been a long and lonely battle. There would be more difficulties ahead, he had no doubt about that. But now he had someone on his side—someone who understood and loved him anyway.

Gracie was already comfortable with Anna. Maybe one day her feelings would deepen into something else, the way his own feelings had deepened, against all his expectations, and despite his best efforts to keep them at bay.

Anna was partly right. Some things were worth fighting for, there was no doubt about it. But maybe—just maybe—for other things the best plan of all was to surrender completely.

And as Anna's lips met his, Connor, his heart soaring, did just that.

To find out more about Sharon Booth and her books visit her website

www.sharonbooth.com

where you can also sign up for her monthly newsletter to get her latest news, cover reveals, release dates, giveaways and more.

Next in the Bramblewick Series

Christmas at the Country Practice

Christmas has arrived in Bramblewick, along with plenty of snow and festive good cheer.

The village is gearing up for the Christmas Eve wedding of popular GP Connor Blake, and much-loved receptionist Anna.

At the Bramblewick Surgery a new GP, Riley MacDonald, is working alongside Connor, and he's proving to be highly efficient and organised.

When Nell Williamson, proprietor of Spill the Beans café and bakery in the village, first sets eyes on Riley, it's love at first sight. Nell has always believed that she would know "the one" when she met him, and she's convinced that Riley is the man she's been waiting for.

Riley, on the other hand, is a hardened cynic. Still humiliated from a broken engagement he's keeping well away from relationships, and is confused by Nell's attentions. Her every attempt to attract him pushes him further away, convincing her friends she's on a hiding to nothing, even though he turns into a clumsy mess whenever Nell's around.

Deciding she's a control freak who should be avoided at all costs, Riley makes a serious error of judgement which could cost her dearly.

As Christmas approaches, best man Riley and bridesmaid Nell are further apart than ever.

Can the two of them reach an understanding before their friends' big day, or will it be the most awkward wedding in Bramblewick's history?